She did a littl

to demonst

Matt caught the scent of her perfume, drifting out alongside the salty brine of the ocean.

He should get out of here. He should take his jacket and go home.

Before he did something really stupid.

"Belle." He stopped. They hadn't gone more than about five hundred feet, but the people back at the site were silhouetted against the sunset, oddly anonymous and far away. He turned toward her. He could just make out her features in the dying light, but, even so, arousal shot through him like a lust-tipped arrow.

"Belle…"

"Yes?" She sounded slightly breathless. He wondered whether she could feel it, too. Something arcing between them, tugging at thoughts they both knew they shouldn't be having…

Dear Reader,

I remember it so well. When I got the call from Harlequin Books offering to buy my first book, I struggled to sound professional during the conversation. Then I jumped up and down like a madwoman, shouting with delight, scaring the heck out of my baby boy, who'd been trying to sleep. "The sale" is a dream come true. And writers know how many people cherish this same dream but never get the call.

That first book, *Sunswept Summer* for Harlequin Presents, was published twenty-two years ago. Since then I have written more than thirty romances, for Harlequin Presents, Harlequin Temptation, Signature Select…and, for the past several years, Harlequin Superromance.

Along the way it turned into so much more than a job. It blessed me with an incredible family of creative people who have become my best friends, my inspiration, my education, my consolation…and my laughter. Harlequin writers are always ready to commiserate or celebrate with one another, lifting a cyber-champagne either way.

Harlequin editors (especially mine!) are sharp as tacks at finding a story's flaws, and yet unfailingly nurturing, never forgetting that our "product" is a piece of our own heart. They make me want to be better.

Harlequin readers are…well, you're the reason we write. You come to our stories with your imaginations full-throttle, and then you take the time to suggest ideas, point out missteps, share your own experiences. You give us the energy to write the next one.

I'd like to congratulate a wonderful company! And I'd also like to thank the writers, editors and readers who have made this career such a joy!

Kathleen O'Brien

P.S. Visit Kathleen at www.KOBrienOnline.com.

For the Love of Family
Kathleen O'Brien

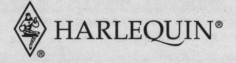

HARLEQUIN®

TORONTO • NEW YORK • LONDON
AMSTERDAM • PARIS • SYDNEY • HAMBURG
STOCKHOLM • ATHENS • TOKYO • MILAN • MADRID
PRAGUE • WARSAW • BUDAPEST • AUCKLAND

To Tara Taylor Quinn, Karina Bliss and
Janice Kay Johnson, who made writing this book
so much fun. And, of course, to Victoria Curran,
who with patience and good humor kept us
all on track. It was wonderful
working with you, ladies!

Recycling programs
for this product may
not exist in your area.

ISBN-13: 978-0-373-71590-9

FOR THE LOVE OF FAMILY

Copyright © 2009 by Kathleen O'Brien.

www.eHarlequin.com

Printed in U.S.A.

ABOUT THE AUTHOR

Kathleen O'Brien was a feature writer and TV critic before marrying a fellow journalist. Motherhood, which followed soon after, was so marvelous she turned to writing novels, which could be done at home. Coming from a wonderfully crazy Southern Gothic family herself, she loves writing about people coping with big, bad challenges and overcoming them with courage, love and a little dumb luck! She fully believes what her older sister used to tell her: "*Normal* is just someone you don't know well enough yet."

Books by Kathleen O'Brien

**HARLEQUIN
SUPERROMANCE**

1015—WINTER BABY*
1047—BABES IN ARMS*
1086—THE REDEMPTION OF
          MATTHEW QUINN*
1146—THE ONE SAFE PLACE*
1176—THE HOMECOMING BABY
1231—THE SAINT†
1249—THE SINNER†
1266—THE STRANGER†
1382—CHRISTMAS IN
          HAWTHORN BAY
1411—EVERYTHING BUT
          THE BABY
1441—TEXAS BABY
1572—TEXAS WEDDING

*Four Seasons in Firefly Glen
†The Heroes of Heyday

**HARLEQUIN
SINGLE TITLE**

MYSTERIES OF LOST
    ANGEL INN
"The Edge of Memory"

SIGNATURE SELECT

HAPPILY NEVER AFTER
QUIET AS THE GRAVE

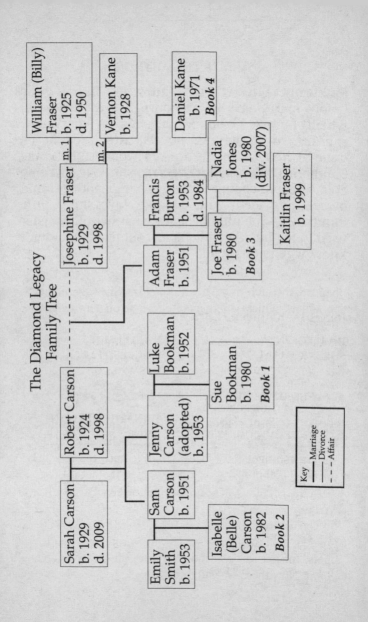

The Diamond Legacy
Family Tree

William (Billy) Fraser b. 1925 d. 1950

Vernon Kane b. 1928

Daniel Kane b. 1971
Book 4

Josephine Fraser b. 1929 d. 1998

Robert Carson b. 1924 d. 1998

Sarah Carson b. 1929 d. 2009

Francis Burton b. 1953 d. 1984

Adam Fraser b. 1951

Luke Bookman b. 1952

Jenny Carson (adopted) b. 1953

Sam Carson b. 1951

Emily Smith b. 1953

Nadia Jones b. 1980 (div. 2007)

Joe Fraser b. 1980
Book 3

Kaitlin Fraser b. 1999

Sue Bookman b. 1980
Book 1

Isabelle (Belle) Carson b. 1982
Book 2

Key
Marriage
Divorce
Affair

CHAPTER ONE

BELLE CARSON PAUSED outside the Yardley Hotel ballroom, trying to work up the nerve to go in. Sucking in her bare stomach, she straightened her black wig and licked her lips, though she could hardly feel them beneath the inch-thick, neon-red gloss. She squared her shoulders, which set the metallic fringe on her tiny gold bra jingling.

A pair of middle-aged ladies strolling through the lobby squinted toward her disapprovingly. Maybe she shouldn't have left her coat in the car. With her costume on full display, the ladies probably assumed she was the stripper for someone's bachelor party.

She should have found their puritanical nosiness funny. It was a measure of how nervous she was that she smiled apologetically and pointed toward the placard the hotel had propped on an easel near the door.

Malone/Trafalgar/Smithers Halloween Party. PRIVATE.

The women relaxed, finally smiling back. They nodded, then idiotically waited, like protective maiden aunts, for her to open the door and get safely inside. *Great.* Now there was no turning back.

Giving the ladies another unnecessary smile, Belle yanked open the heavy door and practically shoved herself inside.

Luckily, the room was packed, and no one noticed her lurching entrance. Under cover of the sound system, which was playing "The Monster Mash," she took a deep breath, adjusted her wig one more time and scanned the room.

Back in her dorm, with her roommate, Pandora, laughing and egging her on, this had seemed like a great adventure. Spunky, creative, fun and brave.

Now Belle wasn't at all sure she could pull it off.

She didn't like to think of herself as a coward. When she was about six, she'd realized she had inherited the doormat gene from her mother, and she'd vowed to fight her fate. She was nineteen now, and in all those years she hadn't once let herself give in to fear, not even fear of her coldhearted, razor-tongued father.

Tonight, though… Tonight was different.

For starters, she'd never crashed a party being held by a total stranger before. She definitely had never tarted herself up in a Cleopatra costume so skimpy it violated decency laws in forty-nine states.

And she had never, ever, ever done crazy stuff like this just so she could chase down and impress a boyfriend.

Speaking of which…where was Andy? She couldn't see very clearly. She'd left her glasses behind on her unmade bed. "Cleopatra didn't wear glasses," Dorrie had said, the gin making the line sound hilarious…instead of just dumb. How could Belle wow and seduce Andy if she couldn't even find him?

He hadn't even told her what he'd be wearing tonight.

In fact, he hadn't mentioned the party to her at all, until she discovered the invitation in his jacket pocket.

"Why should I have mentioned it? You wouldn't ask for the night off, not just to have a little fun. That's your problem, Belle. You don't do fun."

At the time, she'd been furious. How unfair, how illogical was that? she'd asked him. He didn't know what she would have done. She *might* have asked for time off.

Besides, she didn't notice Andy offering to pay her rent, or her tuition, so that she wouldn't have to serve smoothies to rude college kids who tipped in linty piles of nickels and dimes. He didn't even pay for his own. His daddy did, which meant he didn't understand one single blasted thing about Belle's reality. If she'd let her dad pay the bills, he would have attached so many strings she wouldn't have been able to breathe and…

She'd stopped herself before the next word came out. She knew that if she got too "mouthy," as her father always called it, Andy would use it as an excuse to escalate the fight, and they'd probably break up.

So she'd consulted with Pandora, who had suggested this escapade. Andy was losing interest? Andy thought Belle was a bore? Time to show him how wrong he was.

Pandora was a senior, and she had friends in the theater department. They'd raided the costume wardrobe, and two hours later Belle didn't even recognize herself in the mirror.

A dramatic black wig hid her blond curls; kohl liner created exotic black almonds out of her ordinary blue eyes; rubber inserts swelled the skimpy gold top more impressively than her God-given B-cups had any right to look. Not much actual cloth, but everything else shimmered and jingled.

A hip-hugging skirt so low it showed her birthmark, a light brown stain on her right hip, shaped like an inch-long map of Italy. Jeweled sandals, huge rhinestone chandelier earrings, a belt of tinkling gold coins, bracelets and bangles, and a silver snake wrapped around her upper arm.

Trashy? Reckless? Maybe. But definitely not a bore.

The room was huge, and happily chaotic. On the far side, people crowded up to a buffet table that stretched the length of the wall. Across from that, a bunch of kids had lined up for a costume contest. In the center of the room, a few dozen people twirled and laughed, waving their arms in a silly dance.

Belle forced herself to move along the perimeter, laying her hand over her belly to quiet the butterflies. The bare flesh tightened at the touch of her cold fingers. She decided to head for the buffet. Maybe, with a sandwich to absorb the gin she'd had with Pandora a couple of hours ago, she could calm down.

Before she reached the table, she bumped into a middle-aged astronaut carrying an overflowing cocktail in each hand.

After scanning her from head to toe, he extended one of the glasses. "Oh," he said with a loopy grin. "How I wish I'd come as Julius Caesar."

The glass was close enough that the alcohol fumes knifed up her nostrils. She coughed and shook her head, but didn't speak. A forty-year-old man offering a college freshman liquor? Obviously, in this getup, she no longer looked nineteen.

She pointed vaguely to her left, as if she had someone to meet, and made a hard turn in the other direction.

But within thirty seconds, a blond Indiana Jones had slipped up beside her. "Hel*lo*," he murmured, putting his hand on her bare hip. "I do believe I have found the Holy Grail."

Yuck. She hoped he couldn't feel the goose bumps under his fingers. He might think it was chemistry, when actually it was pure disgust. She would have liked to slap his hand away, but she couldn't risk causing a scene. She forced a smile, shook her head again and abruptly peeled off to the right.

Suddenly this seemed like a serious mistake. Her annoyance resurfaced. If Andy was losing interest, then why was she trying so hard to hang on? Wasn't this a little like what her mom always did? Remaking herself in an image more pleasing to the Testosterone God?

Belle didn't really want a boyfriend who didn't appreciate her until she put on a hooker suit, did she?

Did she?

Note to self: Sloe gin fizzes do not enhance decision-making skills.

Just a yard away, a tuxedoed James Bond, complete with slick hair and smarmy smile, was headed toward her, one dyed-black eyebrow raised rakishly. She could just imagine the "Pussy Galore" jokes this guy had up his sleeve.

Belle dodged again, then positioned herself safely

against the least-populated wall. The feathery fronds of a gigantic potted fern shielded her, which might give her time to pick Andy out of the hordes of space aliens, princesses, cowboys, carhops and cavemen.

Maybe that pirate…? No, he was too tall. The Benjamin Franklin? No. Too old.

Then, as if Fate decided to point a finger, one of the catering staff dropped a tray, and several people bent to help gather up the mess. In the space created by the fuss, she saw him.

He'd come as a cowboy, of course, ten-gallon hat and all. His grandfather owned a ranch in Nevada, and he never stopped bragging about it. She could have guessed as much, if she'd been thinking clearly.

But she couldn't have guessed that he'd have his arm wrapped tightly around a fairy princess, a gorgeous woman with platinum-blond hair, gigantic, glittering opalescent wings and gravity-defying breasts bigger than the helium balloons that floated around them.

For a minute, Belle's mind wouldn't put the pieces together. He had said he was coming alone.

He bent down, winding his arm around the girl's neck, and kissed her. The kiss went on so long Belle's own lungs began to feel tight. She knew that kiss, that claustrophobic headlock.

Andy called it his "power kiss." For the first time, seeing it from the outside, Belle recognized it for what it was. A power-*freak* kiss. The only thing that turned Andy on was control.

Finally he let the princess come up for air. Amazingly, she still looked dreamy-faced and adoring. Andy whispered something to her, and the two of them began to walk toward the ballroom doors.

Then they were gone.

As the room whirled oddly around her, Belle tried to figure out exactly what she was feeling. Her knees were weak, and she was slightly light-headed. Mostly she was numb.

Maybe it was too soon to feel anything like pain, the way she might slip and cut herself with a kitchen knife, and see the blood before she felt the sting.

But she definitely already felt the anger. And a searing burn of embarrassment, too. She'd dressed up in this uncomfortable costume to impress that…that lying baboon?

She should go home. What was the point in staying now? But she wasn't sure about her knees, which still felt a bit soupy. The earrings weighed a ton, and the wig was giving her a headache.

Shutting her eyes, she leaned her head back against the wall. The fake hair shifted a fraction of an inch—a weird sensation, as if her scalp were literally crawling.

"Are you okay?"

Her eyes flew open to find a masked Zorro bending over her, a beer in his hand.

God, had she stumbled into the Perverts Anonymous meeting?

"I'm *fine*," she said tightly. "And no, you may not mark me with a Z."

He looked at her a minute, his eyes dark and inscrutable behind that mask. He was nearly a foot taller than she was—six inches taller than Andy, at least. And unless they made falsies for men's costumes, too, he had

an awesome body. Broad shoulders, tight hips and muscles rippling in all the right places.

He wouldn't have to obsess about power, and half
throttle petite females to make himself feel like a man.
He would take control for granted.

He tilted his head curiously, though she couldn't tell
whether he hadn't heard her or didn't understand what
she meant. She narrowed her eyes. Sexy body or no sexy
body, she was sick to the gills of deflecting passes from
all the wrong men at this party.

"Look, I said I—"

Beneath the mask, Zorro's eyes crinkled at the
corners. His mouth curved, revealing even white teeth,
and he began to laugh.

It was, surprisingly, a charming sound. Low, rumbling, manly. Completely uninhibited and genuine. She
wasn't used to that, not in a man. Her father always
chuckled with his lips shut, as if to prove he was still in
control. Andy's laughter—she had never realized this
before—was always too loud and somehow false.

Zorro was obviously accustomed to being happy,
and it hadn't occurred to him to fake it, ration it or in
any way tinker with the feeling.

On the other hand, she might be reading too much into
a sexy baritone and a great pair of shoulders. He might just
be a merry drunk. He might have been tossing back beer
and vodka and anchovies with Mr. Astronaut all night. She
continued to spear him with her gimlet gaze, just in case.

"Sorry," he said, still chuckling. "I was just thinking how disappointed you're going to be when you
see my sword."

"What?"

He touched the hilt. Filigreed silver sparkled at his narrow, ridiculously sexy waist. "It's plastic, you see. All show. I couldn't carve a Z into a pat of butter."

She bit her lower lip, feeling like a fool for assuming his solicitude had been a come-on. Then she felt even dumber, realizing that she was going to have neon-red lipstick all over her teeth. Cleopatra the Blushing Virgin Vampire. *Charming.*

"I'm sorry," she said, running her tongue over her teeth as hard as she could, tasting the nasty wax. "I thought you were…well, it's just that a couple of other guys have…"

He smiled. "I can imagine."

She felt herself flushing. "Nothing creepy. Nothing out of line. Just…flirting. I…I wasn't in the mood."

He tilted his head again, and she could see by the whites of his eyes that he was checking her out, as the others had done, from the black wig to the red toenails. This time, oddly, she didn't mind as much.

"Of course not." His mobile mouth curved. "Still. If you didn't want the men to notice that you're smoking hot, I'll bet that costume store had a nice little nun outfit you could have bought instead."

A nice little nun. Oh, if only she'd done exactly that. In spite of herself, she had to laugh.

"Fair enough," she admitted, fighting the urge to pull her hip-hugging skirt up a bit. "But you see—" she gazed out into the crowd again "—it wasn't *guys* I wanted to impress. More like a guy. Singular."

"Ah." Did she imagine it, or did he sound disappointed? "Anyone I know?"

Oops. She shouldn't have opened the door to questions like that. She had no idea who had invited Andy—the Malones, the Trafalgars or the Smithers. And of course, she had no idea which family, if any, Zorro was connected to.

"I doubt it," she said. "But it doesn't matter. He's not here anymore. I was going to…surprise him. But he's gone."

She realized that a wistful note had crept into her voice. It reminded her uncomfortably of her mom's tone when her dad called to say don't wait up, he would be working late. "When he left, he had someone with him. A panting, top-heavy blonde on a leash. So my costume is actually a moot point."

"He did?" Zorro's eyes lit up. He sighed with feeling, staring down at his beer bottle. "God, I love stupid men."

She hesitated. That was a strange reaction. For the first time she wondered whether he might be drunk.

"Okay," she said. "I'll bite. How do you know he's stupid?"

Zorro leaned his head to one side again. Just a fraction of an inch, but it was lethally cute. She grew subtly warmer.

"False modesty doesn't really go with that costume." He smiled. "You know how I know."

She laughed, though some remote part of her mind wondered whether she ought to be flirting with a new man already. Surely Emily Post would insist that there was some requisite period of mourning, even for a faithless baboon like Andy.

Belle decided that she'd given it at least ninety

seconds, which seemed like plenty. There was something about this guy…

"It is just a costume, though. Underneath all this stuff, I might be…" She hesitated. "Boring."

He shook his head slowly.

"Stupid."

He kept shaking.

"Bitchy."

"Okay, maybe a little. I did notice that you intended to kickbox me into next week if I dared to come too close." He laughed. "But I like bitchy. In the Malone family we call it starch. My grandmother would shoot me if I so much as talked to a woman without starch."

Belle wanted to say something clever, but was momentarily speechless.

He was a Malone?

He liked bitchy?

He wedged the half-empty beer bottle carefully into the dirt of the potted palm. Then he held out his hand. "Dance with me."

She smiled. *He liked bitchy.*

She couldn't have said no if she tried.

She didn't try.

She hadn't realized how late it had grown. The DJ had moved to slow songs, and someone had turned down the lights. As she and Zorro made their way to the dance floor, she noticed that children all over the room were falling asleep over their mother's shoulders, on their laps, across carefully arranged chairs, with their daddy's coats rolled up as pillows.

It felt illogically natural to walk into this man's arms, which were every bit as strong and leanly muscled as she had imagined. He smelled fresh, like limes, with a smoky undercurrent of beer. Now and then her costume jingled softly, a light note under the music.

He was graceful, and he made her graceful, though she had always believed she was a terrible dancer. She felt as light as one of the silver balloons.

They didn't talk until the third song. It was as if they'd already found each other in words, and now they wanted to learn each other by touch. Legs braiding easily, never tangling. Her cheek against his chin, and then, gradually, lowering to his shoulder.

She knew that her lips left a red mark on his shoulder, though it was invisible against the Zorro black. She wondered if he would notice, if he would have it dry-cleaned away tomorrow, when the magic wore off.

"Thank you," he said suddenly, his low voice rumbling against her chest.

She raised her head to look at him. "For what?"

"For this. I didn't expect to be happy tonight."

"Why not?" She glanced around. "It's a lovely party."

His strong mouth was somber, and she realized that, because of the mask that cloaked his eyes, she had learned to read the man's moods by his lips.

"I know," he said. "And I'm supposed to be celebrating. I just got my MBA, and last week I landed a new job. It's a great job. All kinds of zeros on the paycheck, and a corner office with picture windows thrown in for good measure."

She watched him. It didn't occur to her to wonder

why he was telling her this. The intimacy between them might be illogical, but it was real.

"A great job. I guess that means there's a 'but…'"

He nodded. "*But*…I'm an ungrateful son of a bitch, and I don't want it. I feel pretty damn sure that within a year I'm going to sit at that corner window seriously thinking about jumping out of it."

"So don't take it."

For the first time, he missed a step. Their legs came together awkwardly for a split second, and then he recovered. "It's not that simple."

She raised her eyebrows. "Why not?"

"Because nothing ever is." He tightened his arms around her waist and dipped her lightly to a swell in the music. "Except this, right now. With you."

She knew that, as abruptly as he'd begun, he was through talking. And she accepted his silence, because the whole night was strange and magical, and didn't follow any of the rules she'd ever known.

She didn't know him, and yet she felt her soul touching his. She hadn't been invited to this party, and yet she had never felt more at home anywhere. Not even at the house that really was her home.

Especially not there.

They danced two more dances. They kept moving subtly, still entwined, even between songs, when there was no music. The clock was ticking, but she intended to savor every minute she had left.

Finally the DJ announced that the next song would be the last. A sleepy protest went up from the dance floor, from the people drowsing at the tables and the stragglers at the buffet. She had to bite back her own protest, and her Zorro stiffened as if he, too, disliked the idea of midnight tolling.

"Let's get out of here," he said. "Let me take you to my place."

She drew back. She opened her lips but wasn't sure what to say.

He touched the corner of her mouth with one finger. "Don't look like that," he said. "Don't be afraid. You can trust me."

She hesitated. It was one thing to dance with him here, in this ballroom full of sleepy families and silly costumes and a sign on the door that said Private and kept the world at bay. It would be quite another to leave this place with...whoever he was.

Somebody Malone.

Hands on her shoulders, he swiveled her around. "See that gorgeous old lady over there, dressed like Marie Antoinette? That's my grandmother, Angelina. The guy in the bear suit is my brother Red. The ballerina is his girlfriend, Patty, unless she's come to her senses in the past hour and ditched him. My name is Matthew Malone, and, as I already mentioned, my totally unthreatening sword came straight from Toys Я Us."

He rotated her gently, until she faced him again. "If you come with me, I can't promise I won't kiss you. I want that. I want more than that. But I promise I won't do anything unless you tell me it's all right."

She was a fool to consider it, but she didn't care. She didn't care. She felt as if she'd entered this ballroom as a child playing games, and she was leaving it utterly changed. She had never made love to anyone, but she knew it was possible...likely...that she would make love to this man tonight.

To Matthew Malone. It seemed strange to know his name. Strange, too, that he hadn't asked for hers.

Something started to shiver, deep inside. She took his hand and let him lead her to the double doors. They stopped briefly to talk to a handsome man who introduced himself as Matt's brother Colby, but subtly managed not to require her name in return.

The men exchanged a few quiet words, which seemed to be about the car, or perhaps who would be driving. She didn't worry about it. She felt strangely free from worries of all kinds.

By now the clerks at the registration desk must have seen a hundred costumes. No one blinked an eye when Zorro and Cleopatra walked with a quiet urgency through the lobby, hand in hand.

After the warm, crowded room, the San Francisco night air was chilly, but she didn't want to break the spell by stopping to grab her coat out of her car. He put his arm around her shoulder and tucked her up against his chest. Against his warmth...but it made her shiver more.

He bypassed the valet stand and wound through the parking lot's long black aisles, half-empty now, with isolated cars shining under the starlight.

He stopped at a silver sedan.

"Do you mind driving?" He held out a pair of keys.

She frowned. "Drive your car? Why?"

"I shouldn't get behind a wheel. I was drinking pretty hard tonight."

She was surprised. "You were?"

"Yeah. I knew everyone expected me to be wildly excited about the job, and I just couldn't face it sober. A couple of six-packs seemed like the quickest way to get there." He shrugged. "Once I found you, I didn't need it anymore."

Though he'd been holding a beer when she met him, she'd assumed that was his first. He didn't look, talk or dance like a man who was under the influence.

Although…how could she know how he looked when he was drunk? She knew virtually nothing about him, except that he was handsome, and funny and gentle.

And he made her insides turn to liquid silver.

But how many drinks could he possibly have had, and still dance with such seductive grace?

"Too many," he said, as if he read her mind. "It's not something I do very often. Tonight was…a bad night."

A pang of sympathy stabbed her. Underneath the suave looks and easy wit, he was sad. She was shocked by the intensity of her desire to make that sadness go away.

"I'll be glad to drive." Taking the keys from his outstretched hand, she unlocked the doors. "I had a couple of drinks, but that was hours ago. I think I'm okay."

He opened her door, and as she moved to slide in, he suddenly caught her around the waist.

"I wish I'd found you sooner," he said. "You do things to me that no alcohol could ever do."

"I'm glad," she said, feeling the shivers start again. She looked up into his dark eyes, trying to read them behind the mask. She felt deliciously bold, reborn as a woman to whom courage came naturally. "If you're going to be wildly excited tonight, I want it to be because of me."

He groaned softly. He bent his head toward hers, his gaze hard on her mouth. She made a low sound and shut her eyes, waiting for the lovely pressure of his lips closing over hers.

"You have to tell me," he said with a low thrum of urgency. "Tell me you want this."

Couldn't he see that she did? She opened her eyes, knowing they were dazed, unfocused under the heavy Egyptian makeup.

"I want this," she whispered. "I want this. I want—"

And then finally, with a half laugh, he claimed her, driving away the cold air with his hot, hard lips. He covered her parted mouth, indifferent to the red lipstick that she knew would end up all over both of them.

She reached up and threaded her fingers through his hair, bringing him closer. Her lips opened under his exploring tongue, and she felt her whole body opening, too. She was melting, ripening, blooming as if she were a rose in the noonday sun, not a half-clad Cleopatra on a cold October night.

His mouth tasted like mint and beer and sugar cookies, and he filled her with a fiery sweetness. She let go of his hair and ran her hands up and down his back, learning the contours of him, the long lean muscles on either side of his spine, the firm hollows at the small of his back.

It was more than she could stand. She wished they had already reached wherever he was taking her. She wished they could shed these silly costumes and lie together on silky sheets. She wanted to touch the bare skin beneath the black cloth and satin mask.

She could feel his arousal, and she wanted it inside her, though she only half understood what that would really mean.

She pulled away. "Let's go," she said. "Hurry."

He nodded. His lips were almost as red as hers, and the sight was strangely sexy. She reached up to touch their swollen curves, which she'd painted with her passion.

His voice husky, he gave her directions to his house. Then he climbed into the passenger's side of the car. When she turned the key in the ignition, music came on in the darkness—low, murmuring music that wasn't quite wild enough for her mood. But she didn't know how to change it, and she didn't want to waste any time anyhow. So she let it play on.

When she shivered, he dialed up the heater and laid his hand against her thigh, rubbing warmth into the chilled, bare skin. She heard him sigh, and caught the glint of moonlight along his jaw as he tilted his head back and shut his eyes.

Maybe, she thought later, it was Fate, intervening at the last minute.

Saving her from herself.

Or maybe it was just too dark. Or too hot. Or too far.

Or too many beers, finally catching up with even the strongest head.

She'd never know for sure. All she knew was that somewhere in the warm darkness, with the rhythmic purr of the expensive engine and the lulling sound of

Chopin filling the air, the man she had chosen to be her first lover fell asleep.

He didn't wake up when she stopped the car in front of his elegant town house, a three-story brownstone with potted yellow flowers on the stairs. He slept on, his head against the window, when she got out and called a cab from her cell phone.

He didn't wake even when she leaned across the seat and kissed him goodbye.

When the cab arrived, she climbed in and gave the driver the name of the hotel, so she could get her abandoned car. As he streaked away, she allowed herself one last look behind.

She wondered what she would do if the silver sedan's door suddenly opened and he rushed out, calling her name.

But Zorro slept on.

CHAPTER TWO

Eight years later

TWO HOURS INTO HIS grandmother's dinner party, held on the lantern-lit patio behind her waterfront home in Belvedere Cove, Matt Malone could hardly keep his eyes open, even though he had just knocked back a cup of black coffee so thick and strong it could have walked across the lawn on its own two feet.

He stifled a yawn, recrossed his legs and rotated his shoulders.

He hated this point in a party, when the food was eaten and all the decent conversations were exhausted. The women had finally grown tired of pretending to be interested in guy talk, and vice versa.

It was at this moment, when the special-interest groups started forming, that he could always tell whether a Malone-brother relationship had any future. Tonight, the guest list was small. Just the three guys and their dates, and Nana Lina. And, judging by how the women had clustered together as soon as it was humanly possible, not a single brother had a chance of eating Nana Lina's pasta with the same lady this time next year.

Oh, well. Matt didn't care much. Tiffani, his date, was inventive in bed, but she thought she was also a creative cook, and loved to make him pancakes the morning after. She thought she was a great conversationalist, too.

Well, one out of three wasn't bad, but it wouldn't take her to next year.

The summer night was balmy, with a light wind carrying the scent of the Pacific across the grass. The Japanese lanterns swayed from the trees, and the candles guttered sleepily on the tabletop.

His grandparents had bought this house, just over the bridge in Marin County, because Colm loved the water, and Nana Lina wanted space for entertaining. She adored having the whole family gathered around, and, a true extrovert, she knew how to throw a party, and never missed a chance.

Right now she was showing Red's girlfriend, Marie, the purple rhododendron. Marie was oohing and aahing over the flowers. This was her first Malone get-together, and she was still trying to flatter Nana Lina. Colby's date, Stephanie, and Matt's girlfriend, Tiffani, knew better than to bother. Nana Lina might look like an old lady, but was sharp and dangerous as a steak knife, and she wasn't partial to the taste of baloney.

Instead, Stephanie and Tiffani were huddled over the necklace Colby had just bought for Stephanie. These weren't stupid women, so it blew Matt's mind how many ways they could slice the same plain gold chain. Apparently there were infinite variations on the theme. Snake chain, foxtail chain, wheat and rope, popcorn, tinsel and diamond. White gold, rose gold, yellow gold, and every combination of the above, all available to the high-priced crap-maker.

Colby stood with his back to them, staring out at the water, munching a pear and pretending to be deaf. But Matt caught Red's gaze, and knew that he wasn't the only one bored out of his skull. Red grinned and tipped his head a fraction of an inch westward. The message was clear.

The boathouse.

Matt stood up right away and stretched. It was safest to be the first. By the second or third departure, someone might have caught on that this was a breakout. Everyone knew it was the slow fish that always got tangled in the net.

"I was thinking. I'd better go check on that thing. You know, that thing on the boat. Nobody has put any stuff on it in ages, and you never know."

Red rolled his eyes. Okay, as excuses went it was pretty lame, but Matt could tell the ladies weren't really listening, so a clever one would have been wasted, anyhow. He grinned at his little brother and sauntered away slowly. You never hurried. Fast, jerky motions drew attention.

He made his way down the sloping lawns, over the creaking boards of the dock, and then slipped quietly through the open boathouse door. The dim, musky interior was as blessedly silent as the interior of a church.

Only the sound of water lapping against the sailboat, and the invisible plash of a shorebird launching itself into flight.

Instantly, he felt wide-awake again. He flicked on the

bare overhead bulb and settled into the most comfortable deck chair. Another perk of being the first to arrive.

Colby showed up next, and Red followed maybe two minutes behind. Each man entered with a heartfelt sigh from deep in the diaphragm. Forget next year. Those women weren't going to make it to next month.

Colby, the eldest, snagged the next best lounger, leaving Red to make do with the three-legged, moldy-canvas director's chair. They kept meaning to get another solid one, but they never did. Maybe it was too entertaining to try to avoid being the one who got stuck.

Colby pulled three beers out of his jacket pockets and handed them around. "Listen," he said, shaking his head, "if you ever hear that I'm about to buy another woman jewelry, would someone please stop me?"

Red laughed. "How about we just shoot you? You will obviously have lost your mind."

"You're not finished buying geegaws," Matt assured him. "Steph clearly thinks this necklace is an appetizer. She's already drooling for the main course." He waggled his eyebrows ominously. "A big fat, juicy diamond ring."

Colby groaned and popped the top of his beer can with an emphatic sizzle. He had turned thirty-two last month, and women clearly thought he was old enough to start making commitments. Problem was, Colby was as commitment phobic as anyone Matt had ever met, up to and including himself.

Red, at only twenty-nine, could still claim youth as an excuse, although Matt sometimes wondered whether his little brother might be the first to settle down. He loved kids, and wanted one of his own.

But he still had a lot of growing up to do. He was about three-quarters kid himself. As if to prove it, Red picked up one of the antiquated blue darts and tossed it toward the target, which they'd affixed on the far wall about twenty years ago.

Half the fun of boathouse darts was the iron-clad rule that, if your dart fell into the frigid open water where the *MacGregor* sailboat was tied, you had to jump in, fully dressed, to get it yourself.

Matt propped his feet against the wall and rolled the cool beer can across his forehead. He probably wouldn't open it. He didn't drink much anymore. He didn't have time.

As the general manager of Diamante Pizza, his grandmother's chain of delivery pizza franchises, which covered about seventy-five square miles of California coastline, he couldn't afford a slow-motion hangover morning.

Now that they were planning this expansion—which was exciting, exhausting and riskier than anything he'd dared to do before—he was on the road every day. He worked harder than anyone on the payroll, including the delivery guys. In fact, he'd been known to deliver many a pizza, in a pinch. Made plenty of them, too.

He loved all of it. He wasn't the most glamorous CEO in California, or the richest. But he was probably the happiest.

It beat the hell out of that yuppie corner-office prison he'd come within a whisker of checking himself into for life. He'd been only twenty-two, but he'd felt like a defeated, hopeless old man. He still remembered the claustrophobic feeling that had come over him when he'd accepted the job offer, like being buried alive, or smothered in his sleep.

And he still remembered the night he had decided to turn it down. The night the lights came back on in his life. And the mysterious, beautiful stranger who had helped it all come clear.

Red skipped onto, then off, the 26-foot *MacGregor* to get to the other side and retrieve his darts. He had hit everything but the bull's-eye. He came back, set down his beer with a glare, as if it was responsible for his crummy aim, and started over.

"What I can't understand," he said irritably, "is why they need to talk about jewelry so much. I mean, you want to hang a bunch of glittery shit from your ears and your neck, well, hell, it's kind of nutty, when you think about it, but hey. If it feels good, go for it. But do you have to spend all night *talking* about it?"

"What else do they have to talk about?" Colby smiled. "They don't like football."

Matt raised his unopened beer in an affirmative salute. "There you go."

But Red was on a rant, and he was enjoying himself too much to drop it. "I mean, would we do that? Hell, no. I've got a nice gold watch Grandpa Colm gave me, right? Say I take it out, I want to show you. You say, 'Nice watch, bro.' And that's it. Game, set, match, we're done."

Colby shrugged. "It's a girl thing. Like curtains, or slip-covers. You ever hear them get revved up on slipcovers?"

Red turned around. "What the hell is a slipcover?" His eyes widened. "Does it come from Victoria's Secret? Because *that* I could happily—"

Colby tossed his wadded-up cocktail napkin at his little brother. "Idiot," he said affectionately.

"Well, I still don't get it. How the hell do you get emotional about a piece of jewelry? A guy just wouldn't. I mean, okay, there was that one trashy-looking mystery earring that Matt used to sleep with—"

Matt laughed. "I did not sleep with it."

"That's right!" Colby leaned forward eagerly. "He's right. You were obsessed with that thing, man. You did the third degree on everyone at the Halloween party that year, trying to find out whose earring it was." He turned to Red. "But I'm not sure this counts, because it wasn't like normal jewelry. It was symbolic. It stood for all kinds of important stuff."

Red screwed up his face. "Like what? What did it stand for?"

"Sex, of course. Fabulous, sweaty, no-strings sex with a gorgeous stranger." His voice was full of laughter, though his face was deadpan. "Dream sex. The best sex our brother Zorro ever had. Or rather, never had."

"Oh, that's right." Red pulled a fake-pity face. "Poor Zorro. He slept right through it."

"I did not sleep *through* it," Matt said, although he was having trouble not laughing himself. It did sound ridiculous, now. At the time, it had been much harder to take. He had wanted that woman more fiercely than he'd ever wanted any other woman in his life. "The sex part never happened. I fell asleep on the way home, and when I woke up, she was gone. All she left behind was that earring, tangled in my shirt."

Colby shook his head. "That," he said, "is just sad.

No wonder you sleep with it under your pillow. No wonder you keep it, even to this day, locked in your diary, taped on the tearstained page next to the word *Nevermore*."

"Give it up," Matt said. "I don't have a diary. You must be thinking about your own. That pink one? With the lace?"

Red was strangely silent, and Matt suddenly realized that his younger brother was giving him a quizzical look.

"What's the matter?" Matt laughed. "Is the pink one yours?"

"You *do* still have it," Red said slowly. He twisted the dart absently between his fingers. "The earring. I saw something in your valet, when I borrowed your cuff links the other night. I didn't think about it, but now that you mention it…"

"You stole my cuff links, you little bastard?"

It was a decent try, but Matt knew his diversion wasn't going to work. God, he wished he had thrown that damn earring away. He'd meant to, a dozen times over the years. He wasn't even sure why he hadn't. It had sifted farther and farther to the bottom of his valet, until he rarely even glimpsed it, and even more rarely let it cross his mind.

But it was there. And now Matt was never going to hear the end of it. Brothers were worse than Inquisition torturers. Once they got something good on you, that was when the fun began.

"You really do still have it?" Colby looked incredulous. The torture potential of this tidbit obviously hadn't dawned on him yet. "For real? You've kept it for what, eight years? That old piece of toy-store crap?"

They heard footsteps on the dock. Ordinarily, that would have been bad news, signaling the end of their solitude, but right now Matt welcomed any distraction.

The figure that appeared in the doorway was far more daunting than any of the young women. It was Nana Lina, and she stood with her shoulders back and her chin up. They all knew what that meant.

They were in big trouble.

"First of all," she said in her clear, autocratic voice. "I'd like to observe that if you boys are so insecure in your own manhood that you consistently choose to date young women who have no imagination, starch or charm, that is in itself a grave disappointment."

Red put down the darts. "Nana Lina, we're—"

"I'm not finished. And besides, I'm not talking about your date, Red. Marie at least has a real feel for flowers." She turned to glare at Colby and Matt, and Matt knew that neither of them felt a day older than ten. "Secondly, when you feel the need to escape those women, as you undoubtedly will, given that they are, as I said, without imagination, starch or charm, you will *not* abandon me in their midst. I assure you I find them every bit as stultifying as you do, and I don't even get the benefit of having sex with them tonight."

Red was young enough to blush, but Matt laughed out loud. God, she was fantastic, wasn't she? She couldn't have nailed the problem better if she had been able to read their minds. Deep inside, they knew. They were taking the cheap way out, getting great sex without having to put much effort into the relationship—a pretty present would make up for any little oversight or missed date.

Colby laughed, too. Matt leaned over and kissed his wonderful grandmother on the cheek. Then he took her arm.

"I'm sorry, Nana," he said. "Next time we'll bring you with us."

And as they slowly walked her back up the lawn to where Marie, Stephanie and Tiffani were chatting comfortably, not appearing to be particularly distressed by the absence of the men, Matt let the new awareness sink in.

He needed to stop dating girls like this. It was cliché, this laziness, this running away from commitment, running straight into the undemanding arms of bright-enough, nice-enough good-time girls.

He knew better. He'd been raised by a fabulous grandmother, and a brilliant mother, although she had died too young. It was, actually, an insult to those strong role models for him to sleep with women he didn't really, in the bright light of day, even like very much.

Much less love.

Maybe now that the expansion had reached such a delicate point, when so much of the family history, and his grandmother's security, was on the line, he should back off romance altogether for a while. If he got this business move wrong, he wouldn't be able to live with himself.

He felt better just making the decision. Work now. Focus on Diamante, and make sure he protected the treasure his grandmother had entrusted to him.

Maybe later, when he'd earned it, a relationship. A real one, with a woman who had imagination, starch and charm.

He chuckled to himself, and his grandmother gave

him a sharp look. "What right have you to be so pleased with yourself?" she asked acerbically.

"I'm not." He squeezed her arm. "I'm pleased with you."

She grunted, pretending she didn't believe him, but he knew she probably did, and might even be able to guess why. The two of them were simpatico. They understood each other in a special way.

He wondered, not for the first time, what Nana Lina would have thought of the bitchy, beautiful girl with the crystal earring.

How different would things have been if he hadn't fallen asleep that fateful Halloween night?

EVEN THOUGH SHE WAS late to her dinner with George, Belle Carson was using every red light to check the Internet on her cell phone for other employment openings around town.

She was desperate. Over the past month, she'd tried everything from social-networking pages to the traditional want ads. She'd applied for every single job that included the word *writer.*

Copywriter. Ad writer. Freelance writer. Ghost writer. Web writer.

Surely one of them would come through. She saw one for a technical writer, but a blast from the horn behind her pointed out that the light had turned green. She'd apply for that one when she got back home tonight.

Home to the tableful of bills she was almost afraid to open. Home to the apartment she couldn't really afford, now that she no longer had a roommate.

Her cell phone rang as she hit the gas. She glanced at the display. Her dad. She pressed the "ignore" button and kept driving. Ever since the revelation about her grandfather's secret life, her dad's had been snarlier than ever. She'd tried to be empathetic. The news had rocked him, more than the rest of them. It had undermined his sense of his own importance, his special place in the family.

But right now she wasn't up to tending to his wounded ego. He probably just wanted to know how the job search was coming, and he'd hear the desperation in her voice, no matter how hard she tried to hide it.

Desperation. The word seemed extreme, and yet it fit. But was she desperate enough to take the job George Phelps had invited her to dinner to discuss?

She tried to calm herself. Maybe he wouldn't offer the job tonight. Maybe he just wanted to talk. Maybe she'd have a little more time to make up her mind.

It wasn't that she didn't appreciate the life raft George was extending. It was a respectable job with acceptable pay and excellent benefits. But for her it would be a compromise job. Purely a punch-the-clock-and-pay-the-bills job.

She glanced at her phone, wondering if she should widen her search parameters. Was seventy-five miles too far to commute?

But she had reached the restaurant, one of the trendy bar-plus-gourmet-dinner places that had probably sprung up in the past fifteen minutes. Parking was impossible, and she had to use her last cash, a wrinkled five dollar bill, to pay for a valet.

She found George instantly, sitting at a window table.

He was hard to miss, a handsome forty-something who was probably six-foot-six and shaped like a string bean. They had worked together at the *El Marleen Beacon,* and he'd shared his Skittles with her when they both worked the copy desk at night. He'd toss the candy, and if she could catch it she could have it.

George had been laid off in one of the earliest rounds of cutbacks in the newspaper industry. But he had landed on his feet, becoming the well-paid communications director for a rapidly expanding local pizza franchise.

Expanding enough that he was ready to hire an assistant.

He stood as she arrived, bumping his head into the faux Tiffany lamp that dangled over the table. "Hey, there," he said. "You look gorgeous."

She grimaced, returned his kiss, then sat down with a sigh. "You're not at work now, George. You don't have to spin me. My hair looks like a fright wig. I've been in this suit since six this morning, and it's half a size too small anyhow."

He handed her a menu. "I know. That's why you look gorgeous."

She groaned and bent her head over the list of choices. Apparently you could get endive salad, romaine salad, spinach salad and salad–salad.

The waitress presented herself at the end of the table. Belle closed the menu and smiled. "I guess I'll have the salad."

"And a sloe gin fizz." George raised one eyebrow. "Which you'll stir around and around until it's disgusting, but will never drink. If I remember correctly."

She laughed, and waited while he placed his order, too. It was nice, being with him again. He was a lot better dressed than he had been on a journalist's salary, but otherwise, he was the same delightful dork, too handsome for his own good and saved from being a boring yuppie only by the smart-as-hell twinkle in his eye.

"You know," he said as he unfolded his napkin, "I keep hoping that someday I'll get the whole disgusting truth about that sloe gin story."

"Oh, good grief." One very late night at the bar across the street from the newspaper, all the *Beacon* reporters had dissolved into helpless laughter because Belle confided that once, long ago, she'd had a tragic sloe gin fizz experience.

For a writer, she'd sure put that badly. When she made matters worse by earnestly explaining that she ordered the cocktail now just to remind herself that she never wanted to drink another one as long as she lived, the table had exploded.

She'd had to change jobs to get away from the jokes.

She scowled. "Damn it, George. Aren't you supposed to pretend you don't know all that embarrassing stuff? How can we have a proper interview, where I try to impress you with how mature and competent I am, if you keep bringing up all my dirty secrets? Mention the Skittles and I'm out of here."

He sobered. He toyed with his fork and didn't meet her eyes. "Well, are you, Belle? Trying to impress me? Are you interested in the job?"

She bit her lower lip, wondering how to respond. He knew her well enough to guess how little enthusiasm she had for the position. When she first heard that he'd turned to public relations, she had felt sorry for him, wondering what it was like to be forced to play for the other side.

In journalism, PR reps were viewed at best like ants at the picnic, annoying but harmless. At worst, they were seen as sleight of hand artists, slipping the truth under a shell while they got you to look in another direction.

Belle could have gone into PR right from the start. Everyone knew it made more money. In fact, her father, who thought journalism was an underpaid profession that was probably dying, had tried to talk her into it.

But Belle had always wanted to write for a newspaper. Who knew when the seed had been planted? She couldn't remember not wanting to be an investigative reporter, uncovering scandals, standing up for the little guy, facing down the corporate bigwigs, all the clichés.

She'd been preparing for it since her first day of college. You might say she'd spent her whole life preparing for it. Standing up to her militaristic father, refusing to let him get away with bullying the family…it had to be excellent training for the career she loved.

Two months ago, after years of inching her way up, she'd landed her first job at a real daily newspaper. It had been the happiest day of her life.

The idyll lasted a month. Then, after a particularly bad earnings report, management had been told to slash the budget. One month ago, just thirty days after getting her press badge, she and about fifty other people in the paper's newsroom had been laid off.

She'd been job-hunting ever since. But, maddeningly, her father seemed to have been right. Journalism as an industry was struggling. No one was hiring, or if they were, they were hiring people with thirty years experience, not thirty days.

Which was why, when George called her this morning, she hadn't said an immediate, emphatic *no*.

"I'm not sure," she said, deciding to be honest. That they had a happy work history was the most tempting thing about the offer. George Phelps was an ethical man, and it would take more than a PR job to change that.

"I do need a job. Bad. David moved out two months ago, so I'm paying all the rent myself. I had bought a car, too. I thought…I thought I was set at the *Chronicle*. I wasn't thinking I needed a fat savings account to fall back on just yet."

He shook his head. "That must have been nasty. Losing David, then the job."

The sloe gin fizz had arrived, and she found herself fiddling with it, buying time. She didn't want to get into the David story. She hadn't exactly *lost* him. But he was gone, and so was his half of the rent, which was the pertinent part.

"I want to stay in the newspaper business. You know how much it means to me. But I'm just not sure that's going to be possible."

George nodded. "There's an army of ex-journalists out there right now, Belle. You're all knocking on the same closed doors." He looked at her straight. "The door at Diamante Pizza is wide open. I want you there. I think you'd be surprised. I think you'd be terrific at it."

She felt ungrateful, not jumping at the chance. Everything he said was true. And yet she had always been haunted by Zorro's face that night, when he'd told her about the job he felt he had to accept. Kings in a tumbrel, on their way to the guillotine, probably had looked a lot like that.

She still thought about him now and then, especially when she stared down into a lukewarm sloe gin fizz. She always said a stupid little prayer that the job had turned out to be better than he'd feared. She didn't like to think of those sexy eyes gone cold and dead, him staring out that corner window, wishing he had the courage to jump.

She took a deep breath. "I can't say yes yet, George. I'm grateful, really I am. But I've had this dream so long. I can't just—"

She frowned, breaking off. George wasn't even looking at her anymore. He was staring over her shoulder, and his face had changed completely. No longer relaxed and natural. He was already rearranging his posture, his jawline, his eyes, morphing into his professional persona.

"Belle, I'm sorry," he said, talking through a fixed smile. "I should have warned you."

"Warned me about what?" Her back itched slightly from the urge to turn around, but something told her not to.

"I invited my boss. I thought you might need convincing, so I asked Matt to meet us here."

She stiffened. "You did what?"

"You'll like him, Belle. He's a regular guy." George never lost his smile. He was good at this deception game. Too good. She was going to kill him.

"You invited your *boss* to eat dinner with us?"

"No. He's just coming by to say hello, and to answer any questions you might have. I thought it would be—"

"Oh, George, how could you—"

But it was too late to say any more. George was rising, his face alight and his hand extended. "Matt! I'm so glad you could make it. I've been telling Belle how great Diamante is, and all because of your leadership."

God, he was laying it on with a trowel! But, though Belle still intended to wring George's neck later, she couldn't embarrass him in front of his boss. Besides, a self-protective part of her hadn't forgotten that she might, in the end, truly need this job.

She swiveled in her chair, arranging a fake smile that was the mirror image of George's. "Hello, Mr.—"

Oh, my God.

Thank heaven she was sitting down.

Otherwise, she would have tumbled like a rag doll, painted eyes staring, painted mouth frozen in helpless surprise.

She met his gaze, and eight years fell away like one tick of the clock, one grain of sand in the hourglass.

Though she hadn't seen him in all those years, the man who stood before her wasn't a stranger.

Or rather, that's exactly what he was.

A stranger. *Her* stranger. Her masked man with strong arms, an easy laugh and kisses that tasted of beer and sugar cookies. The dangerously charming man who, except for the merciful hand of Fate, could have made off that night with her virginity, her self-respect and, God help her, maybe even her heart.

She wished the room would stop spinning around her.

Because she was about to have a job interview with Zorro.

CHAPTER THREE

MATT HAD ARRIVED AT the restaurant about twenty minutes late.

It was his own fault. He'd stayed at the beach too long this afternoon because he was enjoying the waves and unusually warm water, and, if he was honest, because he dreaded tonight's dinner with Tiffani.

This was the goodbye dinner, and he suspected she knew it. She had to recognize that he'd been calling her less frequently, including her on fewer things…even finding himself too busy for sex.

Privately, he classified his lovers into two groups: the mosquitoes and the barnacles. Mosquitoes were light, easy to brush away when their presence began to irritate. Barnacles clung stubbornly, and were deceptively sharp to the touch.

He suspected Tiffani might prove to be a barnacle.

So he'd ignored the dropping sunlight and kept on surfing until Stony Jones, his surfing buddy today, had finally felt the need to mention the time. Stony knew Matt's plans and, though he sympathized, he also understood that being late to the goodbye dinner just made things worse.

Which it obviously had. When Matt entered the restaurant after his quick shower, his hair still damp at the edges, he'd seen Tiffany sitting at "their" table, looking decidedly miffed. He'd caught her eye and shot her an apologetic smile.

Then he'd seen George, off to the left. Oh, crap. He'd forgotten that he'd promised to stop by and say hello to the new hire. He'd even dictated George's dinner spot, to streamline his own schedule.

He'd held one finger up, silently promising Tiffani this wouldn't take long, and headed over to his communication director's table.

"George!" He put as much enthusiasm into the greeting as he could, given that Tiffani's eyes were boring an acid hole in his back. "Sorry I'm late."

George had risen, smiling with his usual warmth, showing no sign that he'd been kept waiting. George was one of the smartest hires Matt had ever made. For more than three decades, Diamante had been making fabulous pizza, but it wasn't until George took over PR that the hungry hordes had discovered it.

George was the reason Matt felt Diamante was ready for this summer's expansion. So if George wanted a young, out-of-work journalist for an assistant, as far as Matt was concerned it was a done deal.

And he was perfectly happy to stop by and put his blessing on the choice, if it made George more comfortable.

What was her name again? He'd been preoccupied with Tiffani and forgot to check his notes. Darn it…was it Beth? Began with a *B,* surely…

But of course George was too smooth to let Matt flounder.

"Matt, I'd like you to meet Belle Carson," he said. "We worked together at the *Beacon* a couple of years ago. She's fabulous, and I'm hoping she'll consider the assistant job."

Matt shook George's hand, while he took in the woman's springy blond curls and round blue eyes, the slim, girlish figure inside a boring blue suit.

He was mildly unimpressed. She wasn't bad looking...if he spotted her at a party, he'd probably make a point of meeting her. But as a hire? She didn't look tough enough to handle the expansion pace he was planning.

In fact, she looked scared to death.

Her handshake was firm, but her fingers were cold as ice water. Behind her blue eyes, he sensed a mind furiously trying to think of what to say.

Was he that intimidating?

"Hi, Belle," he said, keeping his voice casual, unthreatening. "It's great to meet you. George speaks very highly of you, and his recommendation means a lot to me."

"Thank you." She cleared her throat. "It means a lot to me, too."

He let go of her hand, which seemed to give her a little relief, and glanced at George. He wondered whether this doe-eyed, sweet-faced Belle might be more to George than just a former colleague. Though Matt ordinarily didn't concern himself with his employees' personal lives, he'd always suspected George had an eye for a pretty woman. One player usually recognized another.

But this blushing innocent? He found the idea distasteful on several levels. George was forty-three, and this woman couldn't be more than what…twenty-five, tops?

Plus, it was bad business to bring sex into the workplace. If George was pursuing, and Belle was dodging, things could get sticky.

No, George was too smart for anything that dumb. But something wasn't right here. Belle Carson could barely hold herself together.

She ran her fingers through her curls, as if to settle them down, which she must know wasn't possible. They sprang right back to crazy life. She bit her lower lip, then quickly let go of it, as if lip biting was socially unacceptable.

She was actually kind of adorable, though blondes, especially ones with minimal curves, weren't usually his thing. Still…those hot pink cheeks contrasted against the porcelain of her skin, giving her a Kewpie doll charm.

But this wasn't charm school. It was business. How on earth was she going to handle PR if she couldn't even handle the job interview?

"Any details I can help clear up?" He continued to smile. "Either of you have any questions?"

"No," she began.

At the same time George said, "Yes."

She ducked her chin, deferring to the men, but just as her eyes lowered Matt caught a glimpse of something…spunky. A flash that said she didn't like being discounted.

A decidedly un-Kewpie doll flash. In that moment he wondered if she might deserve another look.

He turned to her, ignoring George. "I hope your lack

of curiosity doesn't mean you've decided against the job already."

"Oh, no," George answered for her. "We hadn't gotten far enough for any decisions. I was just about to tell her what an exciting time it would be to come on board."

Matt nodded. "That's true."

She seemed to be regaining her poise, though she still looked wary. He kept talking, giving her more time to settle down.

"Thirty years ago Diamante began as one take-out Italian restaurant, where my grandmother cooked and my grandfather did the books. Now we have thirty pizza-delivery franchises, all along the California coast. In the next couple of months we're opening twenty new franchises and introducing five new products."

She was finally listening. Her eyes, now that they'd lost their deer-in-the-headlights expression, were intelligent, and she didn't seem to be faking her interest.

"It does sound like a challenge," she said.

"Yes. But it's also a gamble. It's the largest single expansion in the company's history. We're extending ourselves right to the cliff edge for this, and it has to succeed. That's why we need the strongest possible PR team. We have to get the word out that Diamante pizza is the best pizza in California."

"I see." She hesitated. Her eyes narrowed slightly. "*Is* it?"

George made a sound. In a man less controlled and compulsively positive, it might have been a groan. He looked at Belle, sending silent messages with his eyes.

She didn't take her gaze from Matt's. She smiled

politely, but not apologetically. "It's a legitimate question, George. Helping to get the word out about a first-class product is one thing. It's a very different proposition to try to spin straw into gold."

Matt had to fight back the urge to laugh. Yes, this lady had spunk, and she obviously had integrity. George had said she was desperate for work, but apparently she'd have to be a whole lot hungrier before she'd sell out.

Okay. He liked that. He had a quality product, and he ran a tight ship. He could afford to hire people with ethics.

"Have you never eaten a Diamante pizza?"

She shook her head.

"Then of course, before you make any decisions, you must do that." He patted George on the shoulder. "Take care of it, would you? Send plenty, so she can share with her family and friends."

He needed to wind this up. Out of the corner of his eye, Matt could see Tiffani rising. George wouldn't have troubled her—she was used to Matt doing business at all hours. But he should have known she wouldn't sit quietly while he chatted with a beautiful woman.

He saw Belle gaze in Tiffani's direction, too. Then she brought her eyes back to Matt, and he thought perhaps they held a slight hint of disdain. She apparently didn't admire his taste in women.

"I appreciate the pizza," she said. "And I—I want you to know I don't mean to sound ungrateful, Mr. Malone, but—"

"Call me Matt," he said. She didn't like that, either, apparently. She blinked quickly, as if to hide some unflattering thought.

He wondered why he was working so hard to persuade her. Colby and Red would undoubtedly say it was just his frustration at being thwarted. They'd probably applaud this woman for being one of the few who refused to fall at his feet.

She smiled, covering nicely. "I don't mean to sound ungrateful," she repeated, and he noticed that this time she didn't call him anything. "But my decision is a little more complicated than that. The road between journalism and public relations travels only one way. If I take this position, it will almost certainly mean I'll never go back to newspaper work."

Wow. That went straight to the point, didn't it? This woman really had some steel under that baby-doll exterior.

He tilted his head. "You mean you'll be tainted by working at my company? You'll be a ruined woman, so to speak?"

George shook his head and held out a hand, almost throwing himself between them. *Poor guy,* Matt thought, once again feeling the urge to laugh. George undoubtedly thought this interview was going up in smoke, when in fact Belle's show of spine had only intrigued Matt.

"No, no," George said heartily, "of course that's not what she means. She—"

"It's okay, George," she said. "You've put it rather starkly, Mr. Malone. But essentially, yes, that's what I mean. It may be unfair, but that's how ethical newspapers would look at it."

Before he could respond, Tiffani touched his shoulder. She gracefully tucked her hand up under his elbow, staking her claim the way any self-respecting cave-woman would, without words or ambivalence.

"Hi, George," she said. Then she nuzzled Matt's shoulder. "Honey, can't work wait?"

God, he wasn't hosting the goodbye dinner a moment too soon. She was being civilized, but even that annoyed him tonight.

It wasn't fair, but her dulcet tones irritated him, in contrast to Belle Carson's uncompromising candor.

He introduced the two women, out of sorts with himself. "Okay, we'll let you guys eat your dinner, then. George, nice to see you." He turned to Belle. "Take your time with the decision. I don't need my answer until Tuesday."

Her eyes widened. "Tuesday?"

He knew three days didn't sound like much. But he didn't care. Though he liked her spark, if she didn't want the job, plenty of other people would. Former journalists were lying thick on the ground right now.

"Tuesday," he repeated. "I would like to have you on our team, Belle. You have guts. I like that."

A strangely wistful half smile flirted at the edges of her mouth. He noticed that she glanced at Tiffani. "You do?"

"Yes. What I don't like is indifference. If you join us, come with all the energy and enthusiasm you've got. My grandmother's business is at stake. So unless you're one hundred percent certain, your answer ought to be no."

HELL, YES, HER ANSWER ought to be no.

On Saturday afternoon, Belle had promised to drive out to Saint Francis Wood to see her mother. But she drove around for a while first, trying to clear her head, and rehearsing about a hundred ways to say that all-important *no*.

She even wound her way up to Twin Peaks, just so she could assure herself that the For Sale sign on her grandmother's house was still there. Her dad was chafing, already starting to blame the Realtors for the lack of buyers, but Belle secretly hoped it would never sell. She had so many memories there. In her mind's eye, she couldn't picture her grandfather anywhere else.

God, she missed her grandparents. Grandpa Robert would have backed her up a hundred percent about this. He'd know she wasn't ready to give up the dream of being a journalist. She wasn't ready to settle for second best.

And she definitely wasn't ready to work for Matt Malone. To punch a clock as his insignificant peon, his hired hack's charity-case assistant. Answer the phone when his brainless bimbos called, maybe get asked to be a dear girl and run out and buy something nice for a forgotten birthday.

Be a slave to the man who had lived in her deepest fantasies for the past eight years.

And worse still…risk the moment when he looked across the office and, because of some trick of light, finally recognized her.

No. She'd had a stroke of luck last night. He clearly hadn't felt the tiniest tug of recognition, not even a fuzzy shimmer of memory. She wasn't going to push her luck.

Her answer *would* be no.

She'd go home this weekend, as she'd planned, and

they'd eat Matt Malone's free pizza, and then, on Monday morning, she'd call George and say thanks but no thanks.

But the whole thing had left her prickling with nerves.

The moment, straight out of one of her dreams, when she'd turned, and there he was...

And even worse, the moment when she'd seen Tiffani—pouty Tiffani with an *i*, which Belle had guessed even before George confirmed it. The moment when she'd realized that Matt Malone, the laughing, fiery Zorro of that never-forgotten night, was just another obnoxious alpha male who liked his women dumb and gorgeous.

She played the moments over and over in her head, until she nearly went mad. By the time she pulled into the front drive of her parents' house, nestled on a quiet street in the beautiful neighborhood of Saint Francis Wood, she was so tired she almost couldn't get out of the car.

Belle ordinarily looked forward to going home. She missed her mother, and now that Belle and her father didn't live under the same roof—and he couldn't threaten to kick her out every time she annoyed him— they seemed to get along better.

Of course, for the two of them, "better" merely meant that it wasn't World War III every time they came within ten feet of each other. Sam still found his mouthy daughter irritating, and Belle still found herself growing mouthier the minute she set foot in the door, just to show him he couldn't intimidate her.

But she didn't see his car, thank goodness. A golf afternoon? Or just one of those days when golf provided cover for something he didn't want to share with his wife? Whichever, she welcomed a few minutes alone with her mom. She pulled herself together, found her key and went inside.

She dropped her bag in the foyer, studiously ignoring her father's framed display of military medals. All bought, of course, not earned. The collection always reminded her of how much he loved power and control.

She headed straight for the smell of coffee coming from the kitchen. The place had the relaxed air it only got when Sam Carson was out. Her mom had turned on the stereo, and left her knitting basket on the kitchen island, like a bowl of wonderful multi-colored exotic fruit.

"Honey!" Emily Carson said, coming in from the back garden, her hands full of herbs. "I wasn't expecting you for another hour."

Belle dropped her keys on the counter and hugged her, noticing that she looked tired. Her mom's pale skin and hair washed out easily, especially when she was under stress. Belle knew the symptoms well, because her own hair and skin did the same.

After the impossible interview with George and Matt Malone last night, she'd seen a similar ghost in the mirror this morning.

Emily put the herbs in a strainer and spanked the dirt from her hands. "Is everything okay?" Her gaze was sharp, and Belle knew she was noticing the pale cheeks. "Do you need some money? I know job hunting can't be…with this economy…"

"I'm fine, really. I just didn't sleep much last night." Belle looked out the kitchen door to the back drive, which was empty. "Where's Dad?"

The pinched lines around her mother's mouth

deepened. "He's with the new attorneys. He won't work with Stan, you know. He's still…exploring options."

Belle's heart tightened. She plopped on the kitchen chair at the island and propped her head against the heel of her hand. "Still? He just can't let it go, can he?"

Her father had been the king of the family for so long now, the only natural son of Robert and Sarah Carson. Learning that he had a brother—and an older brother, at that—had been difficult. Learning that he would not, after all, inherit the Carson diamond, a gorgeous sapphire-surrounded pendant with a romantic past, a heart-shaped jewel that had symbolized the Carson name for generations, had been intolerable.

He'd consulted a steady stream of lawyers ever since his mother's last letter had revealed everything. He simply couldn't accept being displaced.

Worst of all, he didn't want anyone in his family to accept the new relatives, either.

"That's ridiculous," Belle had said when he ordered her not to talk to her newfound uncle, Adam Fraser. "Like it or not, Dad, these people are family. You can't wish them away. You can't bully reality into being whatever you want it to be."

Sam had looked at her with cold fury. "Obviously not," he had said.

Just two words, but the subtext had been cruelly clear. If he could control reality, he wouldn't have ended up with a daughter as disappointing as Belle.

That was Sam's specialty. With a tilt of an eyebrow, a razor edge in his voice, a curl of his handsomely carved lips, he could slice your heart neatly in two.

Often you didn't fully comprehend the damage until much later, when you began to fall apart.

"You know this is difficult for him," her mother said now over the sound of the faucet as she washed the herbs. But her defense seemed rote, as if she'd programmed herself to say it.

Belle began to pick irritably at the bowl of colored yarn. "It was difficult for all of us. But we're trying to get past it. It's nuts. He refuses to interact with any of them."

Her mother nodded, and though she kept her face focused on the herbs, Belle could see the edge of her mouth. Her lips were so tight they were almost white.

She'd probably die of a stroke before she was fifty. The cost of holding back genuine emotion.

"Can't you talk some sense into him, Mom? Can't you tell him he's being—"

Her mother swiveled her head and gave Belle a straight look. "It wouldn't change anything. It would just stir the flames higher. You know that."

Belle opened her mouth, but shut it again. This was an old debate. She could almost see the tire marks on the kitchen floor, from where they'd gone round and round, year after year.

Her mom hadn't ever understood Belle's defiance. "It doesn't have to be like this, honey," Emily had said a hundred times, stroking her daughter's hand as she fought furiously to hold back wounded tears. The first time Belle remembered them having this discussion, she'd been about nine.

"Why is it so hard for you to back down?" her mother had asked. "Why can't you just let him win now and then? He can't change what you think in your heart. But you could pretend to agree with him once in a while, just to make him happy."

Belle hadn't understood that at nine, and she didn't understand it still. Why couldn't her dad be happy unless everyone deferred to him and pretended he was perfect? It didn't matter how many military medals he collected. He wasn't the general, and they didn't all march in his army.

She couldn't pretend. She wouldn't. No matter what the cost, in tempests, in wounds or in lifelong scars.

Her mother was finished washing the herbs, and she shook the colander gently. Setting it aside, she wiped her hands on a blue-striped dishcloth and sat down at the counter, across from Belle.

"Honey, this weekend…" She paused, picking her words. "Can you just let it be?"

Her mother's face had once been strikingly beautiful. Belle had seen the wedding pictures. Tears always ached behind her eyes when she thought of at how vibrant and alive Emily Carson had been at that age.

The years with Belle's father had drained her, as if she'd been living with a vampire. Today, she was so pale, almost translucent. Belle could see blue veins in her cheeks and throat, as if someone had stroked the tip of a pen across her skin. How tiny they were, far too fragile to fill a whole human being with life.

And then the air reverberated with something like thunder as her father's oversize black SUV rumbled into the back drive. Her mother registered the sound, then stood up quickly. Belle wondered whether the sin was sloth, sitting at the kitchen table when she should have been working on dinner, or fraternizing with the enemy—Belle.

"Mom." She caught her mother's hand and squeezed it, wishing she could squeeze warmth into the chilled fingers. "I'll behave. I will. I'll try to get along."

She meant it. She'd suddenly realized how unfair it would be to breeze into town, get her father riled up and then depart again, leaving her mother alone to handle the fallout.

"Thanks, honey." Emily smiled, then turned to the cupboard and pulled out her father's favorite mug. "I hope the coffee's still warm."

Sam entered the kitchen like a gust of cold air. He used just a hair too much force on the door, and its glass panes rattled as it banged shut. Belle took a deep breath. She remembered that sound all too well. It meant her dad's day had been tough, and someone would have to be sacrificed to restore his balance.

She looked at her mother, placidly pouring coffee, like well-trained hired help. And she wondered…if things didn't improve, how long would her mom stay?

"Hi, Dad," Belle said, moving forward to give him a hug. "I'm glad you're back."

"Isabelle. You're early, aren't you?" He returned her hug, but, as usual, he was ready to quit before she was. He touched his finger to his own temple, indicating her glasses. "You really should wear your contacts, Belle. Those glasses make you look like a spinster librarian."

Moving away, he dropped his briefcase on the countertop and took the cup of coffee from his wife's hand. He sipped at it, scowled briefly to register that it had grown lukewarm, then leaned against the countertop, sighing.

"I'm leaving Ackerman," he said to his wife. "Morons. Two hundred dollars an hour to watch them sit around on their thumbs."

Emily, busy washing the decanter so that she could prepare a fresh pot, made a noncommittal sound, which seemed to satisfy him.

He turned to Belle. "How's the job hunt coming?"

"I've had a couple of nibbles," she said, mentally thanking George for making it possible to say that without lying. "Nothing firm yet."

"If it's not firm, it's phony. Don't count on it. Keep looking."

It was the same mantra he used to mobilize his sales force at the dealership. She'd heard it a million times through the years, and she didn't actually disagree with it. But why couldn't he assume she was smart enough, adult enough, to know it without being reminded?

She took a breath. He was trying to help. She was just being prickly. She was defensive because she was only too aware of that pile of bills on her kitchen table back at the apartment.

"I know." She smiled and offered up one of his favorite lines as an olive branch. "Close only counts in horseshoes."

He smiled back. "That's my girl. You'll find something. Just don't go beating your head against brick walls." He pointed the coffee mug toward her to emphasize his point. "The newspaper business is dead. Bury the poor thing before it starts to smell."

"I guess so," she said, searching for a safer subject. Sooner or later he'd remind her that he'd predicted disaster in her newspaper career all along. And she'd say that she would rather have tried and failed than sold out at the start.

And from there things would get ugly.

Her mother came to the rescue. "Nora called while you were gone, Sam. She said it wasn't urgent, but maybe you should…"

Brilliant, Belle thought. Nora was her dad's secretary. She idolized Sam, and could always be counted on to stroke his ego when no one else would.

He shook his head. "She got me on the cell phone on the way back from Ackerman's. Those bastards. You know what they said? 'The law is hazy on this point, Mr. Carson.' Have you ever heard anything more absurd? If only Mitch Taylor was still practicing. This new Wilson guy is a charlatan."

Mitch Taylor had been the Carson family attorney for years, retiring after Belle's grandfather's death. The new lawyer, Stan Wilson, had in Sam's eyes "betrayed" them by letting Sarah bequeath the Carson diamond to Sam's sister, Jenny. A sister he'd always felt comfortably superior to, because she was adopted. It had completely messed with his sense of the universe to learn that Jenny was actually Robert Carson's daughter by blood, as well as by adoption.

To have her inherit the diamond he'd always believed was his birthright? Impossible. He had vowed to overturn it.

"I wonder if they're in cahoots with Wilson. I bet he got to them somehow. Or else they're idiots." He knocked back the last of his coffee. "Too bad you couldn't hang on to David, Belle. It would be mighty useful right now to have a lawyer in the family."

Belle lowered her eyes. With stiffening fingers, she started to rearrange the yarn in her mother's basket, pinks all together, then blues....

"I never will understand what happened there." He let Emily pour him fresh coffee, but he didn't skip a beat. "I mean, you've dated some losers I was glad to see the tail end of, but David was the cream of the crop. A lawyer, good-looking, good money. Hell, if you'd stuck with him, you wouldn't even have needed a job."

Pink, blue, green, yellow.

"I couldn't stick with him, Dad, unless I agreed to marry him. He gave me an ultimatum, remember?"

He laughed. "Yeah. An ultimatum that came attached to a four-carat diamond ring. You're the first woman in history to run screaming from the sight of a ring that size."

She glanced toward her mother, trying to signal that she was sorry. But she just couldn't go on like this. Didn't her mother see what happened when no one stood up to him? It was like feeding the monster in your closet. He didn't go away. He got bigger and hungrier, and it took more of your flesh to satisfy him.

"I don't give a damn how big his ring was, Dad. I didn't want to be his wife. Do you really want a lawyer in the family so badly that you'd have me sell myself to a man I didn't love?"

Her father's face tightened.

"You loved him enough to live with him, and sleep

with him, and let him pay half the rent. There are only two names for women who do that, sweetheart. One of them is *wife*."

Emily made an anguished noise. "Sam—"

"No. It's true. She's pretty mouthy for a young woman who doesn't have anyone to pay her bills, and no prospects for getting a job. I hope she doesn't think she's going to move back into this house."

Belle scraped her stool back. "Don't worry, Dad. I'm only here for the weekend. If I can stand it that long."

She plucked her keys from the countertop. She smiled at her mother, trying to control the shaking she felt moving through her body. "I'll be back in a few minutes, okay?"

"Where are you going? A bit thin-skinned, aren't we? Can't take a little truth?" Her father's cold amusement followed her out to the hall.

Ignoring him, she picked up her purse, and as she went through the front door she was already fumbling for her phone.

She dialed the number wrong twice.

But finally the call went through.

She heard George's voice saying, "hello."

"George? It's Belle." She took a deep breath, leaning against the front porch pillar for support. "If the job's still open, I want it."

CHAPTER FOUR

WHEN MATT'S OFFICE door was open, as it almost always was, he had a direct view of the new hire's cubicle.

The spot used to belong to the director of communications, but George had moved over one desk when Belle Carson came on board. He apparently wanted his assistant to be the first face visitors glimpsed, after the receptionist. Belle needed to meet people, he said. Be visible, make contacts. Integrate.

Matt never micromanaged if he could help it, so he had just nodded. Belle would make an excellent first impression on guests—her manner was much warmer and more appealing, actually, than Francie's, the woman who sat at the reception desk and doubled as office manager.

But now, only two days after Belle's arrival, Matt was wondering whether she might be a little *too* appealing. He hadn't understood a word of the lease he'd supposedly been reading for the past twenty minutes. He'd been too distracted by the way she dangled one shoe from her pink-tipped toes while she talked on the telephone.

He dragged his attention back to the lease. What the hell was wrong with him? He didn't look at his employees' feet. He didn't look at his employees at all, *that way.*

But the navy-blue pump jiggled up and down, at the edge of his peripheral vision, and he found his mind wandering again. Did she fidget like that every time she made a phone call? Or did it mean she was bored, or nervous, or annoyed? She'd been quite reluctant to take the job. He still wasn't sure what had changed her mind.

So maybe the bouncing shoe meant she hated networking with the media, which George undoubtedly had her doing this first week.

"You got a minute?"

Matt jerked his eyes upward, belatedly realizing that George stood in the doorway.

"Sure," he said. He tossed aside the lease gratefully, yawning. "Why is everything lawyers write so damn boring?"

George smiled. "Guess you'll have to ask your brother that one." He hesitated a second, then closed the door behind him.

Matt sat up a little straighter. George knew Matt preferred transparency in all transactions. For Diamante, the "open door" policy wasn't just a sound bite. What was up?

The older man chewed on the inside of his lip a minute, as if trying to decide how to begin. "Have you heard from Bill Duncan?"

Matt frowned. He heard from Bill Duncan, the owner of several small radio stations in outlying municipalities, only twice a year. Matt got invited to Bill and Marcy's Christmas extravaganza, and he got hit up for donations to their Summer Fun charity auction. This was only June. The auction wasn't for another month, at least.

"No. Why?"

"You probably will." George glanced out the glass wall of Matt's office, toward Belle's desk.

Matt looked, too. Belle had put her black glasses on top of her crazy curls and was rubbing her eyes. Then she stood, wandered to the coffee area in the corner and began pouring herself a cup of Francie's coffee.

Matt wondered if she knew about Francie's coffee.

He turned back to George. "Come on, just spit it out. Why will I probably hear from Bill Duncan?"

"Because…well, Belle…" He hiked up his pants a little. "I had her sending out media e-mails yesterday. You know, introducing herself, making nice, saying a few flattering things about the contact, about his work, or you know, whatever compliment she felt comfortable—"

"And?"

"And she wrote an e-mail to *Jim* Duncan. But she sent it to Bill."

Matt absorbed that for a beat, then groaned. Bill and Jim Duncan, no relation, were both media types around town. Unfortunately, they were on opposite sides of the political spectrum, one a business reporter and the other a fat-cat station owner. They hated one another like poison.

"Damn it. *No.*"

"Yeah." George looked miserable. "She had done a helluva job, too, saying how much she admired Jim's work. It was her best letter yet, because apparently she really does like the guy's writing. Unfortunately, she stuck the wrong e-mail address on it. It went to Bill."

As if on cue, Matt's phone rang. He let it ring over to the reception desk. He and George exchanged a glance, but after a few seconds Francie approached the glass wall and tapped on it. She batted her eyes and touched her cheek flirtatiously. It was their code for Tiffani.

Matt shook his head emphatically. This made the fourth call from Tiffani since they'd broken up ten days ago. Each time, he considered relenting—it felt brutal to refuse even to be friends. But he knew a man couldn't leave any chinks in his defenses with the Tiffanis of the world. If she saw a crack in the fortress wall, she'd ooze right through it.

Francie nodded, obviously pleased with Matt's resolve, and stalked back to the phone. George's face was studiously blank, the perfect employee pretending not to know what was going on. Matt appreciated the professionalism, though he was well aware that no one around here had much liked Tiffani.

George cleared his throat. "So, about Bill Duncan…"

"I can handle Bill." He wasn't crazy about the man himself. If Matt ended up getting scratched off the Christmas list he could live with that. "I'm more worried about Belle. Can she cut it, do you think?"

George nodded, still promoting his new hire as vigorously as he ever promoted Diamante Pizza. "Absolutely. She's going to be great. She's got wonderful instincts. I filled her in on the Diamond Sweepstakes yesterday, and she had some inventive ideas."

Matt was glad to hear it. The Diamond Sweepstakes had been Nana Lina's idea. Because Diamante meant diamond, she'd decided to promote the company's sixtieth anniversary expansion by giving away a three-karat diamond solitaire worth sixty thousand dollars.

Everyone who ordered a pizza in the next three

months would automatically be entered in the contest. They'd been running TV and print ads already, created by an outside agency. It was a huge expense, and frankly, Matt thought it was a huge gamble.

But when Nana Lina wanted to do something, Matt got it done.

"Really," George went on, "Belle's a natural. I'm going to have to watch out, or you'll end up giving her my job. She's smart, and friendly, and credible. She's got a sort of natural elegance that—"

It couldn't have been timed more perfectly. Just as George mentioned "elegance," Belle took a sip of Francie's coffee.

Instantly, she choked, coughed and spilled coffee all over her chest. She recoiled in horror. Her glasses tumbled from her head, and her shoe fell off her toes, so that when she stood, wildly brushing at the hot, brown liquid on her white blouse, she lost her balance and had to grab the back of the chair to keep from going down.

The chair rolled, pulling Belle two feet outside her cubicle, before bumping awkwardly into the wall. She stood there, her fair skin flushed as bright as her toenails, as Francie burst into laughter.

George moaned.

"You really should have warned her," Matt said, struggling to hold back his own amusement. Though fifty-five and worked to the bone, Francie was attending night school to get her law degree, and hadn't slept in about six months. She existed on Diet Coke, dark chocolate and coffee that would strip the lining of your esophagus like cheap wallpaper.

"Matt, honestly, today looks pretty bad, but Belle's going to be fine—"

"I know she is. Now get out there and fix the mess. If the poor woman gets any redder, her face is going to explode."

George hustled out. Matt stayed behind his desk, ignoring the urge to jump up and join the rescue mission. Belle was probably dying of embarrassment, and having the brand-new boss hand her a towel wouldn't help matters much.

Besides, he knew himself fairly well. The urge to go out there and soothe this pretty, flustered young woman was way too strong. All day, she'd seemed like a lost kitten, which made him feel sad, because he remembered the spark and sizzle he'd glimpsed in her eyes at the restaurant the other night.

She was a proud woman, and a capable one, but she was out of her element here. It must have been difficult for her to agree to take the job at all. He didn't want her to feel humiliated only two days into it. He didn't want her to feel defeated already.

He found himself wanting to do something gallant, something manly and tender.

But he stopped himself.

Manly? Tender? That darn sure wasn't in the job description of *employer.*

In fact, that was the textbook definition of *hell no.*

ALL MORNING Belle had been a bit uncomfortable about the lunch she'd agreed to have with her newfound cousin Joe today. The invitation had come out of the blue, a real surprise, considering how steadfastly Joe had been ignoring Belle's own overtures. The sudden about-face made her nervous.

When she finally heard the sweet little chime of the lobby elevator announcing Joe's arrival, she moved like a criminal making a prison break. She grabbed her purse and hustled Joe back into the elevator without introducing him to anyone.

Though he'd always been a close friend of her cousin Sue's, Belle had met him a couple of times before, at the reading of the will and at the hospital when his dad had a stroke, so they were hardly on intimate terms. She would have called Sue to join them, but Sue had just returned from a quickie wedding in Vegas and was up to her ears in the red tape of adopting her husband's infant niece.

It was only one floor down to the ground level of the renovated town houses that served as Diamante Incorporated headquarters, but the elevator ride seemed to last forever. Though she had buttoned her jacket over the ruined shirt, the aroma was enough to make anyone gag. She gave Joe a point in the "nice guy" column because, even as the air grew close, he had manners enough not to grimace.

Of course, he knew almost nothing about her, either. He might just think she had terrible taste in perfume.

She crossed her arms, trying to hold in the odor. "So…I don't know the neighborhood all that well yet. Did you have a restaurant in mind?"

There must be plenty of choices. Diamante's location on a shady street in Lower Pacific Heights was an eclectic blend of retail, restaurants, offices and condos. In any two-block segment of this neighborhood you could find almost anything on earth you wanted.

Joe, who seemed to take up a lot of room in this mahogany-paneled box, smiled politely. He had deep-set, dark blue eyes—and the smile didn't quite reach them. "Well, Diamante Pizza is here…the whole first floor, right?"

"Oh, no, no," she said without thinking. "I mean…not that their pizza isn't wonderful. It's just that I would like to *really* get away, you know? Not even think about the job for a while."

"Okay." He shrugged those double-wide shoulders, clearly indifferent to the lunch location. "I saw a couple of restaurants across the street. Mexican and…something else."

"Mexican sounds terrific," she said gratefully. Finally the elevator doors opened, and she escaped into the open air. "Let's see…it's…oh! Banditos? Yes, that looks fine."

She wished she could stop talking. But, combined with the missteps at work, Joe Fraser's quiet demeanor had begun to get on her nerves. He was attractive, with that black hair that looked as if it could be lush if he'd ever let it grow, and those shoulders. But he also had a cowboy's square jaw, and a nose that might have been broken somewhere along the way, which gave him an intimidating edge.

And the few times she'd seen him, at the reading of the will and at the hospital when his father first had the stroke, he'd been giving off no-nonsense vibes. She wondered once again why he'd asked her to lunch in the first place.

Obviously it wasn't a sudden gush of familial warmth.

Now that she was free of Diamante and the maddening awareness of Matt Malone, she felt herself steadying. Maybe Joe had just needed time to adjust to the idea of his new relatives. After all, her dad hadn't exactly welcomed him into the family with open arms.

She could have told him that her father didn't understand the concept of "open arms." But that would have been gratuitous disloyalty, so she waited to see what Joe had in mind.

For a couple of minutes they just sat making small talk, and ordered the same cheese enchiladas, salad and tea. Finally, when the waitress left, Joe scraped his chair closer to the table and cleared his throat.

"I want to talk to you about your mother."

Belle sipped her water, trying not to reveal how surprised she was. She'd been fully expecting him to say he wanted to talk about her father and his rotten attitude. She'd been mulling it over all morning, trying to figure out how honest to be.

But her mother? This was a bit of a shock.

She didn't respond right away. It was a technique her first editor had taught her, back in her college newspaper days. If the reporter talks, the subject doesn't have to. If the reporter rushes to fill the gaps, he never gets any quotes to fill the pages.

Joe fixed his sharp-eyed gaze on her, unblinking. "I guess you know your mother has come by to visit my father in the hospital."

Belle put her glass down carefully, not sure her suddenly shaky fingers wouldn't drop it. Her mother had visited Adam Fraser? It couldn't be true. Her father had given them both explicit orders not to associate with any of the Frasers.

Belle was perfectly willing to defy Sam when he was being a fool or a bastard, or, as was so often the case, both. Otherwise she wouldn't be here right now, eating enchiladas with Joe.

But her mother? Her mother didn't believe in defiance. Emily Carson had grown up with an alcoholic father and a runaway mother, and she had learned early to be a peacemaker. She never challenged Sam. Never. She simply didn't have the courage. It had been bred out of her by her own father.

Joe's eyes narrowed. "You weren't aware of this?"

Apparently Belle needed to work on her poker face. "No," she admitted. "I wasn't. In fact, I can't believe that she…that my father…"

This time her cousin waited, as if curious to hear how she'd phrase it.

But what could she say? *I can't believe my father would allow it?* Joe would think she was crazy. Who could believe, in this day and age, that any man would forbid his wife to speak to his own brother, just because the brother was illegitimate?

Or that, if he did, his wife would bow to his demands?

Belle shook her head, giving up. "Are you absolutely sure?"

"Of course I'm sure." He waved his hand. "I was there when she came."

Belle was disappointed—and a little offended—by his curt tone. Apparently his reluctance to get together hadn't been just nerves or caution. He obviously was just as determined as Sam to dictate a distance between the two sides of the family.

"Okay. She went to see your father." Belle hesitated. "My *uncle*. Is that a problem?"

"Yes, frankly, it is." He speared a chunk of lettuce, though he didn't eat it, and then set his fork down again. "That's why I wanted to talk to you. I hope you can persuade her not to do it again. My father can barely speak. His condition is fragile. Your mother's visit upset him."

Upset him? Belle felt as if she'd been slapped. How could her cousin contend such a patently ridiculous thing?

"That seems unlikely," she said, hearing the same curt tone sharpening her own voice. "My mother is the most sensitive person I know. She considers it her mission in life to make everyone happy. Even, sometimes, when it's not in her own best interests."

"Not in her own best interests?" Joe raised an eyebrow. "Meaning that Sam won't approve."

Belle tilted her chin. "Meaning that it's complicated. But if she's been to see Adam, I guarantee you she has the best of intentions. She always does."

Joe shook his head. "You're going to have to defer to me on this, Belle. I know my father. And, if you'll forgive me, I know *your* father. If he finds out that your mother has been to the hospital, God only knows what he'll do. Which may be what your mother is after."

"What? You think she'd use your father to…"

But he wasn't listening. He leaned forward, and in spite of herself Belle instinctively drew back.

"I haven't a clue what she'd do. Listen, Belle. I don't have anything against you or your mother. I assume you've been as blindsided by all this as we have. But my father and I don't need to get caught in the middle of whatever is going on between your parents. Right now I can't afford to let anyone slow his recovery."

His expression had grown dark, as if he grappled with some emotion too intense to share. "I'm sorry to be rude, Belle, but I'd like you to talk to her. I'd like you to make sure she doesn't come again."

LATER THAT NIGHT, while her best friend, Pandora, drowsed with her baby in the armchair, offering occasional lazy comments, Belle tried on every dress she owned and tried not to panic.

But panic was definitely nibbling at the edges of her psyche. Her first formal staff meeting at Diamante was tomorrow. Matt Malone presided over the sessions, and George had warned her that she'd be expected to have ideas for the upcoming product launch.

She'd been racking her brain all afternoon. Now she was racking her closet. After her missteps today she had an awful lot to prove.

And very little to prove it with. She hadn't come up with any brilliant ideas to suggest, and the closet…

Journalists simply didn't have the same dress code as public relations people. She had one decent suit, and Matt had already seen her in it twice. Even if it hadn't been in an airtight bag ready to go to the dry cleaners, she couldn't have worn it again.

She held up the last of her options, a black sweaterdress that fit well and looked fairly stylish. She caught Pandora's eye in the mirror. "Maybe?"

"Maybe if you were going to a funeral." Her friend's chuckle was soft, but the sleeping baby sprawled out across her chest stirred. Pandora put her hand on little Mary Isabella Anderson's back, and the baby calmed instantly.

"Sorry," she continued in a softer voice. "But bo-ring. Don't you own anything that says 'watch out, world, here I come!'?"

Belle tossed the sweaterdress onto the bed, along with all the other rejected outfits. "My bikini, maybe. Want me to wear that?"

Pandora, whose own wardrobe was always fabulously flamboyant, sighed. She propped her feet on the edge of the bed and studied her rhinestone-encrusted sandals thoughtfully. "Maybe I have something at the theater that would—"

"No." Belle held up a warning palm. Pandora taught drama to high schoolers, and she was famous for having the most elaborate costume department in the entire San Francisco public-school system. "Don't even think about it, Dorrie."

Her friend scowled, ready to argue, but then her face relaxed into a smile. "Oh, right. That didn't work out so great last time, did it? Yeah, you'd better not go the costume route. You wouldn't want Zorro…I mean, your *boss*, falling asleep right in the middle of the meeting."

Ignoring the jibe, Belle dropped onto the vanity chair and stared at herself in the mirror. She looked tired, her face too pale and her eyes shadowed. It wasn't just the job, though of course that didn't help.

These days, almost everything seemed to be going wrong.

The breakup with David, the newspaper layoffs, the money problems that just wouldn't quit. Her father's temper, the strangely hostile meeting with her new cousin, and now this weird news that her mother was acting out of character.

A lot of seemingly unconnected bad karma. But sometimes Belle thought all the ripples could be traced back to the one heavy stone that had been dropped into their lives.

It had all begun the night her adored grandmother died. Or, to be more exact, the morning the will was read, and her equally beloved grandfather's double life was revealed.

Things had begun to go sour that very day. Like some kind of cosmic payback for all the Carson sins and secrets.

Belle tried hoisting her unruly curls into a chignon, but it made her look younger. With a sigh, she let them fall, and gazed at Pandora's reflection again.

"You met my grandfather, Dorrie. Would you have imagined he was capable of something like this?"

The advantage of having a true old friend was that she could follow even the most illogical segues.

Unfazed, Pandora shrugged. "Depends on what you mean by 'this.' Could I imagine he was capable of fathering a couple of kids out of wedlock? Sure." She rubbed her cheek against little Mary's downy head. "Who isn't?"

Belle smiled. Though Pandora had agonized every day of her pregnancy, second-guessing the decision to be a single mother, the arrival of Mary Isabella had answered all those lingering questions. Pandora had been instantaneously bewitched.

She shifted Mary higher onto her shoulder. "But would I have believed he could shut the illegitimate children out of his life, refusing even to acknowledge them? No. I'm still trying to wrap my mind around that one."

So was Belle.

Grandpa Robert's death, when she was only seventeen, had been the single greatest loss of her life. He'd been everything to her…hero, confidant, advisor and safety net. He'd been the wise, patient father figure that Sam Carson simply didn't have the temperament to be.

Losing him once had been hard enough. But now, ten years later, when she learned the truth about his life, it was as if she'd lost him all over again.

"I wonder if Joe is feeling the same way." She put her chin in her hand, still talking to Pandora in the mirror, too tired to turn around. "If he was close to his grandmother, and suddenly he learns that she was some strange man's mistress…that his grandfather isn't his grandfather…that he has an aunt he never knew…"

"Yeah. Kind of a nightmare. Guess you have to cut him some slack for being cranky, huh?"

Belle nodded. They were all in the same boat. They were all looking into the cherished family albums and suddenly seeing only strangers smiling back.

"But let's tackle one problem at a time." Pandora settled Mary into her carrier carefully, so as not to wake her. "We have to get you dressed for tomorrow's performance." She stood in front of the open closet, hands on her hips. "So they dress pretty spiffy over at the pizza palace, huh?"

"They sure do, at least the ones who meet the public. I swear, even the office manager wears Armani."

"And Zorro?"

"His name is Matt, darn it." Belle shook her head. "You don't want me to slip up and call him that in the office one day, do you?"

Pandora rolled her eyes. "As if you could be that dumb."

Belle appreciated her friend's confidence. She wished she shared it.

Her gaze slid to the black velvet shadow box she'd hung over her vanity eight years ago. It held the one remaining crystal earring.

She'd never taken it down, partly because it was so pretty, sparkling and glimmering like caged starlight. Also, though, she kept it partly as a moral parable. The tangible representation of the dangers of pure animal stupidity.

Though she considered herself a smart woman, something about Zorro had lulled her self-preservation instincts into a trance.

She wasn't completely sure he didn't have the same power today.

With a growl of triumph, Pandora yanked a pair of black velvet slacks from their clips and, tossing them over her shoulder, began picking through the remaining items, looking for a shirt.

Belle felt her anxiety receding. If anyone could make

this mishmash of casual junk into something impressive, it was Pandora.

"So…" Pandora considered, then rejected a green gypsy shirt with smocked cuffs. "Does Matt wear Armani, too?"

"He's the exception, I guess. He's got this jacket that probably costs a month's rent. But he puts it on over jeans." She smiled in spite of herself. "Fantastic jeans."

Her friend chuckled and glanced knowingly over her shoulder. "Ho, boy. I have *got* to get a look at this guy."

Belle wrinkled her nose sheepishly. Pandora had heard it all, eight years ago, so there was little point in pretending to be immune to Matt Malone's charms now. "You won't believe it, Dorrie. I had begun to wonder whether some of what I remembered was…you know…"

"Pheromone hallucinations? Lust blindness? Gin-induced hysteria?"

Belle laughed, and felt a little better. In spite of Pandora's constant financial struggles, and now the baby to support, with no father in sight, her indomitable practicality and wit improved any situation.

"Well, it was *your* gin, as I recall," Belle reminded her. "But yeah, I wondered whether some of the sex appeal I remembered was…artificially enhanced. You know. 'Objects you see in your memory are less romantic than they appear.'"

Pandora grinned. "But not this one, huh?"

"Nope. Unfortunately. But at least there's no risk of ending up in bed with him this time around. Not without my Cleopatra costume. He's obviously one of those men who always date bimbos named Trixi with an *i*.

Bambi, with breasts out to here. He wouldn't have looked at me twice without the padded bra."

Pandora laughed, just loudly enough to wake the baby, who whimpered adorably.

"Here," she said, thrusting out the black velvet pants, a shimmery royal blue blouse and a little black bolero jacket Belle had forgotten she owned. And, right on top, a pair of cherry-red pumps, the signature Pandora flair. "It's not Armani, but you won't disgrace yourself."

Belle took the clothes. No, she wouldn't. And if she could just come up with an impressive idea for the product launch…

She could. And she would.

They were already running a diamond sweepstakes. Maybe there was some way to tie into that.

She clutched the clothes to her chest and made herself a vow.

She'd stay up all night if she had to, but she would *not* go in tomorrow without the best damn PR idea Matt Malone had ever heard.

CHAPTER FIVE

THE NINETY-MINUTE meeting was nearly over, and Matt noticed that Belle Carson hadn't uttered a peep.

She looked terrific today, much less like a scared kitten than she had yesterday, but she might as well have been mute. George had tried to draw her out a couple of times, but she'd deflected him with a murmur and a smile.

Thank goodness Nana Lina had decided not to attend the meeting after all, Matt thought. His grandmother had resisted the idea of a public relations department in the first place. She held the purist's view that if a product was superior, it would speak for itself. Matt had spent at least a year overcoming that.

If Nana Lina met Belle today, she would be sure that Matt had hired a pretty face with no brain behind it. That was something he had always refused to do in his professional life, and, though Colby and Red laughed when he'd announced it, it was now something he would refuse to do in his personal life, as well.

The era of the Tiffanis was over.

Unfortunately, with the expansion bearing down on them, he had no time to pursue a woman of substance and develop a relationship of substance, so that pretty much meant the era of sex was over, too.

At least for a while.

He'd heard that some men got a physical thrill out of obsessive work. He hoped to heaven that was true.

"Okay, let's talk about ideas for the launch. We've got exactly three weeks before the new foods are on the menus and the doors open at the new franchises. George, do you have the stats?"

Of course he did. He was both smart and thorough—a one-man marketing and PR whiz. Thank God that stupid newspaper had let him go. Matt wasn't sure he could have tackled this expansion without George to back him up.

George folded back the cover of the oversize pad he'd perched on the easel at the front of the conference room, perfectly positioned so that the light from the bay windows illuminated it.

The first sheet was an organized list of interviews scheduled, ads placed, commercials in the can and ready to air. Matt had already seen the commercials, but the rest of the employees hadn't, so George queued them up on the projection screen.

From there, George walked them through graphs of expenditures, pie charts of market share, and the return expected on each. He handed an updated calendar to Matt, and set aside a copy for Nana Lina, who was scheduled to speak at several appearances and even take a handful of interviews, if Matt could actually talk her into doing so.

"That's it for me, I think. But Belle has another idea,

one she sketched out to me this morning. I think it's an excellent one."

George sat down and smiled at his protégée. "I'll let her tell you about it."

She had obviously been dreading this moment. She wasn't naive enough to actually gape, but Matt imagined he could feel the thrill of anxiety that raced through her veins. He had to give her kudos. She put a charming smile on her pretty face and stood up gracefully.

"I'm not sure it's necessarily an idea you'll want to pursue, particularly as we only have a few weeks before launch. It would require a significant man-hour investment."

"Okay. I'll keep that in mind."

She nodded, picked up a few papers from the table in front of her and glanced over them without appearing rushed or flustered. She'd certainly shed the gauche insecurity of yesterday rather quickly. George watched her like a proud but anxious parent.

Matt had to admit he liked her poise, too, especially since he still imagined he could feel her fear lying not far beneath. He didn't think less of her for that. Only fools felt no fear when they faced the unknown. It was how you handled it that mattered.

And he liked that she'd said "we." "*We* only have a few weeks." Either she'd already emotionally invested herself in her job, or she knew how to parse her pronouns.

She swallowed and brushed her blond curls over one shoulder. She had been holding on to the back of her chair, but now let go.

"George has filled me in on the Diamond Sweepstakes you've got planned. It's a wonderful campaign."

"I'm glad you like it." Matt hadn't intended for that to come out as sardonic, but she blinked quickly, and the tips of her cheekbones suddenly looked pinker.

"Yes, well. My idea would expand on the Diamond Sweepstakes." She adjusted those square black glasses, which were obviously designed to make people take her more seriously. Offset the sexy Kewpie doll look.

She clearly didn't know they just drew attention to the amazing china-blue eyes behind them.

"As I understand it," she said, "to celebrate the opening of your new franchises, and the launch of your new menu items, you're giving away a diamond ring as the grand prize. Everyone who buys your new product, Cinnamon Diamond pastries, in the first ninety days is automatically entered in the sweepstakes."

"Yes."

She took a deep breath, as if she had a lot of information to get out in one swoop. "Okay. I thought perhaps we could capitalize on that campaign by holding individual events to celebrate the opening of your new franchises. At these events, we would give away an order of Cinnamon Diamonds with every pizza purchased. These pastries would be specially prepared so that some have toy rings folded inside. Anyone who finds a ring will get an extra entry in the sweepstakes."

Her words sounded slightly rote, as if she'd memorized that little speech and practiced it in front of the mirror. She took a second deep breath when she finished, clearly relieved to have it out.

"Interesting." It actually was a fair idea, if expensive. Launching any new product required a lot of word of mouth. But that was hard to come by, unless you could get the food into a lot of mouths in the first place.

"Where would the events be held?"

She smiled, finding her rhythm. "I noticed that each of your new locations is a beach town. This couldn't be a coincidence. These spots were chosen because that's where Diamante's customers are. So let's go to the beach. The atmosphere is casual, fun, natural—the image Diamante has always promoted. Sun, surf, healthy young people and families having a good time. Visuals that will particularly appeal to television viewers."

"You said we'll be giving away the Cinnamon Diamonds free? That'll cost us quite a bit, won't it?"

"Yes." Reaching across the table, she handed him a sheet of paper on which some rough calculations had been printed. Preliminary figures, but Matt could see that it was an educated guess, and it was a damn big number.

"Rather ambitious," he said. "But perhaps we can recoup some of this with additional pizza sales?"

She shook her head. "I don't think that would be advisable. As you probably know, newspapers normally refuse to cover purely commercial events. We need another angle. I feel fairly certain that if you donated part of your profits to some local charity, perhaps to education or the environment, you could overcome that reluctance."

George had begun to look fidgety, which was interesting.

"Part of my profits? What percentage were you thinking?"

George twitched, but Belle met Matt's gaze straight on. "A hundred."

Matt laughed, and a low hum broke out among several of the other managers seated around the table. "You want me to donate a hundred percent of the profits to charity?"

She didn't blink. "Yes."

"Really, Miss Carson." Todd Kirkland, who handled Diamante's charitable Driver Compensation Fund, broke in, his voice subtly condescending, as if he thought he could teach the new girl a thing or two. "I'm in favor of charity. That's the sum total of my work at Diamante, in fact. But even I… Doesn't that seem a little overreaching?"

Belle turned politely, facing him with the same undaunted expression. "No. Not if you want newspapers and television stations to take the event seriously. If they stay home, then we might as well do the same."

Francie, who had never cared for Todd, scowled. "I think it's a fantastic idea," she said, a shade aggressively.

Then she glanced at Matt, shrugging. Apparently she'd appointed herself Belle's guard dog.

Or it might just have been the caffeine.

Belle smiled at the older woman, then turned back to Matt. "In the end, it will cost far less than the price of comparable paid advertising, which is your only alternative."

Matt nodded. "Okay. Is that all?"

"That's the broad outline." She started to pull out her chair, but hesitated at the last minute. "There was one other thing."

George watched her carefully. Apparently this part was unscripted.

Matt tilted his head. "Yes?"

"It would be most effective if you attended the events yourself. Optimally, you would personally serve the pizza."

"Really? Why?"

"Well, I've been researching the company, and, in terms of narratives that are useful for public relations, Diamante Pizza has two choices. One is your grandmother, who created the pizza you sell today. The other is…you."

"Me?"

"Yes. You are your grandmother's heir, the one who will carry the business into the future. You are her claim to immortality. And, of course, you're…"

For just a minute her poise broke, and he thought he saw her blush under the carefully applied makeup.

"I'm what?"

She lifted her chin slightly, clearly deciding to go for the gold. "You're telegenic. Wear swim trunks, and the TV stations will eat it up. You won't be able to bake enough Cinnamon Diamonds to keep up with the demand."

Matt looked at George, who was staring at Belle as if she'd just won him the Kentucky Derby. Apparently, even he hadn't realized exactly how much grit the filly he'd adopted had inside her.

Matt cleared his throat. "George?"

The man beamed at him. "Yeah?"

"You like it?"

"I love it." George stood. "Well done, Belle. Inspired…" He nodded, clearly at a loss for words.

"Okay, then." Matt began gathering up his papers, ready to get back to work. He had six properties to walk through this afternoon, and he wanted to get to Nana Lina's for dinner. "We'll do it."

Belle's brows drew together slightly. "What?"

"I said we'll do it."

As the others filed out of the conference room, chattering about the controversial new developments, she just stood there. She clamped her hands across the back of the chair again, squeezing the leather so hard her knuckles turned white.

He paused at the door. "Everything okay, Belle?"

"When you say we'll do it…" She looked at him as if he'd spoken in another language she was trying hard to decode. "You mean, you'll think about it?"

He laughed. Clearly, in all her plotting and rehearsing in front of the mirror, she hadn't ever seen beyond the challenge of making her pitch. She hadn't fully understood that there would come a moment when she had to turn the idea into reality.

"I've already thought about it. I like it. Now it's time to get it done."

SHE MUST HAVE LOST her mind.

By the time Belle got back to her desk, her knees were as shaky as Jell-O. What had she been thinking? Why had she come up with such an elaborate scheme to launch these silly Cinnamon Diamonds? Couldn't she just have suggested putting flyers on cars, or a coupon in the paper? Or anything simple that she would have had a hope in hell of pulling off?

But no, she'd felt the need to get brilliant. Determined to impress Matt, she'd gotten drunk on her own creativity, fallen in love with her own clever ideas.

Well, this would teach her to show off. Now she had to actually make this happen.

Watching Matt confer with George in his office, she had the queasy feeling that he had approved her idea primarily to test her. To see whether she was anything more than hot air and window dressing.

Well, was she?

Guess it was time to find out.

She turned on her computer and began feverishly looking up wholesale novelty distributors. Just her luck, it would probably be too late to order enough of the plastic diamond rings, and she'd bankrupt this sixty-year-old company overnight.

She was so absorbed in her research she barely heard the elevator chime behind her. She didn't turn around.

But as Belle heard the voice of the visitor, a slow tingle made its way up her spine. The smooth, beautifully modulated tones could belong to only one person.

"Good morning. How are you today? I'm Sam Carson. I'm here to see my daughter."

Belle's fingers stilled on the keyboard. She hadn't seen or spoken to her dad since she'd stormed out of his house ten days ago. Since before she took the job.

And yet he had found her here.

He sounded as if he was in an upbeat mood, but you couldn't tell with him. He was always charming to underlings. They were no threat to him, and he enjoyed their innocent admiration. Plus, he was smart enough to know that even an underpaid porter still controls the key to the gate.

He'd met his match in Francie, though. She wasn't charmed by anyone. As far as Belle had been able to determine, Francie didn't admire any male creature on the planet, with the possible exception of Matt.

"Good morning, Mr. Carson." Francie's Midwestern twang suddenly turned every bit as New England uppity as Sam's, and equally autocratic. "I'm sorry." Belle heard the rustle of pages in Francie's desk calendar. "Is Belle expecting you?"

Oh, dear. Belle swiveled quickly, well aware that her father's charm was so thin it couldn't withstand a Francie attack.

"It's okay," she said, adding a smile to let the other woman know she appreciated the attempt to guard her from unwanted interruptions. "I'm off the phone." She stood. "Hi, Dad. Is everything okay?"

"Well, I'm not sure." He glanced around. "Is there anywhere we can talk privately?"

Belle thought quickly, her gaze going to the office where her two bosses still sat, reviewing sheaves of paperwork. She couldn't really leave right now, three hours before lunch. No one punched a time clock here, but she hadn't been around long enough to gauge how strict Matt was.

Francie touched her arm gently. "The conference room isn't being used. I think there's even some fruit left on the tray from the meeting."

Belle smiled gratefully. "Thank you." She moved toward the opening to the next set of offices. "Dad, we can go in here."

Diamante's small corporate headquarters had originally been three separate town houses, George had explained on the first day. The remodeling had deliberately left the flavor of the original 1890s structures.

The conference room ran along the southern wall of the center town house, a large, lovely space filled with light from two bay windows overlooking the street below. From here she could see Banditos, the Mexican restaurant where she and Joe had eaten yesterday.

Oh, God. That was it, wasn't it? Her father wasn't here to give her grief about her job. He must have found out about her mother's forbidden visit to Adam.

With her stomach starting to churn in that old, familiar way, Belle led her father into the room, which hadn't yet been cleaned up. A few plates with picked-over grapes and kiwi fruit littered the table. The whole office complex always had a faint, delicious odor of pizza from the restaurant downstairs, but the scent was strongest in this room.

Sam wrinkled his nose. "What a mess." He flicked a forefinger, lifting one of the plates. "They don't exactly run a tight ship, do they?"

She could have explained that they had held a long breakfast meeting in here just five minutes ago, but why bother? She'd expected something like this. Having won the newspaper-versus-public-relations argument, he would now have to find something else to criticize.

Obviously the new complaint would be that the firm

that had employed her wasn't big enough, prestigious enough. That it was sloppy, and smelled like a back alley in Little Italy.

Well, to heck with that. Diamante Pizza was an honest, well-managed family business, and Matt Malone had been willing to give an untried neophyte a chance.

That was good enough in her book.

Belle leaned a hip on the edge of the conference table, signifying that their visit would be short. She folded her hands in front of her. She wasn't looking forward to this, but they might as well get it over with.

"Tight enough that I probably shouldn't have personal visitors on his time. What's wrong, Dad? It really couldn't have waited until I got off work tonight?"

"Don't worry. I won't keep you long. I know you must be very busy."

He was being sarcastic, of course, but instead of being hurt Belle found it just plain annoying. He didn't have a clue what she was doing at work today. In his head, she was still nine and trying to sell him a buttercup full of mud stew.

"Yes," she said matter-of-factly. "I am quite busy. But if it's urgent, of course I have time."

"It's about your mother."

Belle kept her expression neutral. She wished she had made the effort to call her mom last night and find out what was going on. But she'd been so wrapped up in preparing for today's meeting. She had foolishly assumed there was plenty of time.

How had her father found out so quickly?

Surely, if her mother had visited Adam, she would

have been careful. It was hard enough to imagine Emily disobeying one of her husband's direct edicts. That she'd do so without covering her tracks was unthinkable.

Maybe Joe had told him. Her cousin had seemed disappointed that Belle wasn't more sympathetic, and they'd parted on chilly terms. Had he decided it would be smarter to take care of the problem himself? Had he left their Mexican lunch and headed straight for Sam's office to warn him to keep Emily in check?

"What about Mom? Is she all right?"

Sam paced to the window, and in the bright sunlight Belle could see about a dozen lines she'd never noticed before. They all pointed downward. Frown lines. Anger lines. And maybe, she was willing to admit, disappointment lines, too.

She'd probably put a few of those there herself.

"No, she's not all right. She's being unbelievably stubborn. I've tried to reason with her, but—" he wiped his hand across his face "—she won't listen to me."

"About what?"

"About anything, frankly. But the most important thing is this whole insanity about the Carson diamond. Everyone knows it has belonged to Carsons for three generations. Everyone knows that's where it was supposed to stay. If your grandmother did anything else, that alone proves she wasn't in her right mind."

Belle slid off the table. She hadn't heard this argument before, and it chilled her all the way to the pit of her stomach. "Grandmother Sarah? Not in her right mind?"

A deep furrow etched the skin between her father's eyebrows. "That's right. She probably had been getting weak in the head for a long time, but we just didn't recognize it. Obviously, though, she was no longer thinking straight."

"Dad." Belle put her fingertips on the table to center herself. "You know that's not true."

Sarah Carson's final illness had been blessedly brief. Up until a week or so before she died, she had remained a steady source of wisdom and comfort for her whole family.

He flushed darkly. "Your mother told you to say that, didn't she?"

"Of course not."

"What the hell is the matter with you two? Are you feeling sorry for those interlopers? Why should we? That woman…how do we even know their story is true?"

"It wasn't *their* story. It was Grandmother Sarah's story."

"The ravings of an old woman. Decades of jealousy and paranoia coming to life in some twisted, senile fiction. Believe me, your mother will probably say the same things when she's old and living in fantasyland."

Belle didn't answer that one, looking away from him to stare at the middle distance.

No matter what happened, no matter how often he was seen with other women or caught in places he had no business being, Sam had always played the aggrieved husband, the martyr whose wife was prone to "imagining things."

Once or twice, through the years, Belle had tried to make him own up to his infidelities. At age eleven, she'd even ridden her bike to his golf club just to prove

to herself that he wasn't really there. But those moments had always backfired. For a few weeks afterward, her father had stayed home more, but he'd made
her mother pay dearly, with incessant demands and a
hair-trigger temper.

Pretty soon, Belle had seen the problem. Her mother
could either leave him or let him do as he pleased. For
some reason, Emily preferred to stay. So, for her sake,
Belle had eventually adopted her mother's posture and
let the charade play out unchallenged.

"Belle, look." His voice grew more conciliatory, but he
jammed one hand in his pocket and fisted it there, so it was
clear the frustration hadn't subsided. "Do you think for
one minute your grandmother would leave the diamond
pendants to anyone but me? To anyone but a Carson?"

Belle smiled wryly. "Aunt Jenny is a Carson. By
adoption and, as it turns out, by birth."

That was the last straw, as she'd known it would be.

With an impulsive growl, he reached out and grabbed
her wrist. "Damn it, Belle, what's wrong with you? Has
someone from their side gotten to you? Have they
turned you against me?"

He held on so tightly Belle's arm ached. She stared
at him, unable to believe this was happening. No matter
how he had belittled or offended Belle and her mother,
he had never laid a hand on them.

Belle had always assured herself that physical abuse
would have been the tipping point. If he'd ever slapped
her, or shaken her, her mother would have packed up
and moved out.

Now here it was, the moment of violence. Had the

revelation of his father's secret family caused him to come completely unstrung?

"Please let go of my hand," she said. "You're hurting me."

"I want an answer, damn it—"

"Belle, can you join George and me in the office for—" Matt stood at the double doors, which she'd left ajar. "Oh, I'm sorry. I didn't realize you were busy."

Her father's hand opened instantly, releasing the arm Belle had been trying to pull free. Surprised, she had to step back an inch to keep her balance, and she felt her cheeks burning.

Her father turned, face still ruddy, but somehow managing a smile.

"I'm sorry," he said with an admirable attempt to sound sheepish and endearing. "I'm Sam Carson. Belle's father. You must be Matt. I shouldn't be keeping her from work, I know. I just needed to steal her for a minute. A small family matter."

Matt leaned one shoulder against the mahogany door frame. "No problem," he said equably. His manner was as easy and laid-back as ever. But his eyes on her dad were flinty, lacking any warmth. She had a feeling this interruption had been manufactured.

"I should go, Dad," she said, trying not to feel sorry for him. But she knew that, under the confident facade, he was probably mortified. This had been an aberration, after all. He didn't manhandle her routinely, though that was probably how it appeared to Matt. "I should get back to work."

Like magic, Francie appeared at his elbow. "Mr.

Carson?" Her voice was mellifluous and deferential, but the signal in her outstretched hand was unmistakable. "I'll be *delighted* to show you out."

Sam had little choice. The best he could do was to appear as if he wanted to leave, anyhow. "Okay." He glanced at his watch. "Look. I'm late already."

He reached out and gave Belle a hug that was obviously for show. Even so, he couldn't bring himself to make it last longer than about one and a half seconds. "Call me later?"

"I'll try." She couldn't promise that she would. If he wanted to continue haranguing her about Grandmother Sarah's mental competence, she wasn't interested. It was a lie, and it would shame them all if he tried to pursue it.

Matt went along with Francie and Belle's father back into the lobby, probably to make sure he didn't refuse to get on the elevator at the last minute. Belle couldn't bring herself to join them. She stayed in the conference room, glad of a few seconds to compose herself.

Rubbing her wrist, she stared down into the street. After a minute or two, she saw her father striding to his car, which was parked half a block downhill from the Diamante building. His movements were rigid, his body stiff. Not an encouraging sign.

"Are you all right?"

She looked up. Matt had returned to the conference-room door. "Yes, I'm fine. I'll be right there." She started to move.

He shook his head. "No, stay if you like. There's no meeting. I just thought you might need…" He smiled. "An exit strategy."

She wasn't sure what to say, but his smile was so infectious she found herself returning it, in spite of everything.

"You were right. I did. Thank you."

It seemed inadequate, as if he deserved a real explanation, so she tried to construct something that would be honest without stringing the family's dirty laundry up for all to see. "My grandmother died recently, and things... things have been very mixed up. My father's a little upset right now, but I'm sure it won't happen again."

"Belle..." Matt hesitated a moment, and then, as if on impulse, moved into the room and joined her at the window. The bay wasn't very big, and it brought them close together, closer than at any time since that night eight years ago.

She found herself staring at him, registering every tiny change. He didn't look older, exactly, though of course he was. He just looked more complicated. More real.

His thick, dark hair was shorter these days. But in the bright light, she could see the same gleaming luster—in the one wave that tickled his forehead, in his brows, in his lashes, even in the hint of stubble dusting his strong jaw.

His body was more sculpted, with more interesting angles, as if he'd shed any lingering immaturity. His face was more powerful, too, the cheekbones more pronounced and the nose more chiseled.

The sunlight picked up a few lines that had been lightly sketched across his golden skin. These eight years must have been happy ones, she thought. Around his eyes, tiny creases fanned upward, like the shadow of a thousand smiles. And on either side of his sensual mouth...not deep grooves of bitterness, like her father's, but subtle hints of dimples, as if his face had been designed for laughter.

She realized suddenly that he was studying her, too. She wondered what he thought of what he saw, and prayed that it wouldn't ring any old, forgotten bells.

The silence stretched several seconds. She scoured her mind for something to say to break the odd tension that had inexplicably arced between them.

"I really am sorry about…all that." She tried to relax her shoulders. "But you don't have to worry. I'll explain to my father that I can't deal with personal issues while I'm at work."

"What?" He tilted his head, as if he didn't remember what they'd been talking about. The memory of him doing the exact same thing in that Halloween ballroom tugged at her midsection.

"Oh." He chuckled. "Look, Belle. I'm not sure George has explained how we operate around here."

"George was very thorough. And I met with HR the first day to—"

"I don't mean paperwork and benefits." He hesitated, as if hunting for the right words. "I mean the unspoken rules. You know? All those little personal details that make the difference between loving your job and dreading coming to work in the morning."

"I do love my job."

But the skepticism on his face made her smile. He obviously hadn't forgotten how frank she'd been that night at the interview.

"Well, okay, that may be an overstatement. But I certainly don't dread it."

"I'm glad," he said. "But I want you to understand that you don't need to apologize for your father coming by. This is your career, not your prison. We will work you damn hard, but we're always a team. With the possible exception of Francie, we're not robo-people. We know that occasionally everyone needs to check on their kids, take their mom to the doctor, eat pizza at their desk."

He grinned. "In fact, we *hope* you'll eat pizza at your desk."

She laughed, but it sounded strained even to her own ears. Oh, God, that smile was so…

For a piercing moment she saw a different man in front of her. She saw the young Zorro, rippling muscles of newfound manhood covered in black satin, with a long, sparkling sword at his side.

The vision sucked the words right out of her mouth.

"When you're here, you can see anyone you like," he continued. "But…if you *don't* want to see someone…"

He let the sentence dwindle. His gaze had slid to her left arm, and his message was clear. She tugged surreptitiously at the sleeve of her jacket, just in case. Her father hadn't been terribly rough, but her fair skin bruised so easily.

"I understand," she said. "And I appreciate it. All of it. Thank you."

She moved awkwardly out of the window bay, needing a little distance so that she could catch her breath and regain her perspective.

It was silly, how warm and protected he could make her feel. No wonder she'd fallen at his feet all those years ago.

Forget how intimidated she was about the product-launch events.

The real challenge of working for Matt Malone would be preventing herself from falling for him all over again.

CHAPTER SIX

"HOW ABOUT THIS ONE?" Belle's mother, who had wandered away to a display rack of summer fashions, held up a white cotton dress with a full skirt and a daffodil-yellow jacket. "It's professional, but has a dash of sex appeal."

Belle looked up from the collection of navy, mauve, black and brown blazers she'd been halfheartedly flipping through.

"No. No sex appeal," she said firmly. "My job is to sell pizzas, not myself."

"Nonsense." With a soft chuckle, her mother brought the dress over and, folding the hanger down, held it under Belle's chin. Emily squinted, considering intently, then sighed. "I don't know. Maybe matching your hair color is a touch precious."

Belle shook her head and pretended to renew her interest in the blazers. But now they looked even more dreary. She'd caught a glimpse of herself in the mirrors, which seemed to be everywhere in this upscale department store. The yellow dress had looked terrific. Light, feminine…and her mother was right about touch of sex appeal.

Especially if she wore her contacts…

She growled under her breath, annoyed with herself. *No. No sex appeal.*

Not when she was at Diamante Pizza. Not when she was around Matt Malone.

Her mother slid the dress back onto the rod and kept looking. After a minute, Belle joined her there. She'd invited her mom along on this shopping trip for two reasons: Emily Carson had better taste than anyone Belle knew, and she wanted a chance to talk to her alone.

Her mother draped an elegant Prussian blue sheath over her arm, then continued flipping. "How many different outfits are you going to need?"

"How many do I *need?* Or how many can I *afford?*" Belle laughed. "I need at least four. We'll have twelve different beach events, but they don't all have media overlap. I figure I can get away with wearing each outfit three times."

She grabbed the dangling price tag of the sheath and held it up for her mom to see. "At this price, I could afford exactly...zero. Come on. We need to find the sale rack."

"Belle." Her mother hesitated. "I'd like to help. To buy you a few things. It would make me happy to see you in—"

"No. Thanks, Mom. Honestly, I appreciate it, but this is my responsibility." Belle eased the blue sheath from her mother's arm and slipped it back onto the rod. She smiled. "And I can handle it. As long as we shop from the sale rack."

Her mother cast a longing look at the blue dress. "If it's about your father..." She lowered her voice. "We don't need to worry about that. I've got some cash from…well, from times when I didn't need quite as much for the housekeeping."

She touched her purse conspiratorially. "He doesn't ever have to know."

Belle recognized an opening when she saw one. She had intended to talk about this over coffee after the shopping, but she had to grab the chance that presented itself.

She took her mother's hand.

"Speaking," she said, "of things Dad doesn't know…"

Her mother's fingers tensed. If Belle had needed confirmation, that involuntary reaction was plenty.

"Joe Fraser came to see me the other day. We had lunch. He said you went by to see his father in the hospital."

Once again Belle was struck by how different her mother was whenever she got away from the house and Sam Carson's repressive influence. Out here in the world Emily Carson was a smart, capable woman. Nothing remotely resembling a doormat.

She didn't blush or try to change the subject. She just sighed, then nodded.

"Yes, I did. I didn't tell you, because I was hoping I wouldn't have to drag you into it. It could get quite uncomfortable, if your father finds out. You know he doesn't approve."

"Yeah. That's an understatement."

Her mother smiled. "I didn't plan to do it. I found myself near the hospital, after the museum board meeting. It suddenly occurred to me that if Adam Fraser were to die in there, I wouldn't be able to live with myself. He deserved better from this family, and if your father couldn't apologize for his behavior, then I could do it for him."

For a minute, Belle didn't know how to respond. The first feeling that came through was an instinctive prick of guilt that she hadn't done the same.

"How was he?"

"Weak. But clearly on the mend." She absently stroked a stack of folded sweaters. "I think I like him. I think we could have been friends, if we'd met under other circumstances."

Belle wasn't so sure. "He seemed awfully quiet at the reading of the will, and he and his son don't seem to have a very warm relationship. As you say, though, it might have been the circumstances."

"I see the tension, of course. He's had a hard life, and it's taken a toll." Another gentle stroke of the sweater, as if it were a kitten, or a child. "But I also see a lot of regret in those eyes."

Belle's stomach tightened. She felt the truth of her mother's comment. Adam Fraser was a complicated man, and had undoubtedly known pain, disappointment and loneliness. Who knew what kind of strange family life this abandoned son had known? He didn't seem to have learned much about love. He had no wife…and anyone could see that his relationship with Joe, his own son, was strained.

Her mother was always the first to understand the human need behind the facades. She was always the first to reach out and forgive.

And this was the woman Joe Fraser had accused of "upsetting" his dad.

"I'm glad you went, Mom."

Belle decided on the spot that she was not going to try to prevent another visit. Joe could do his own dirty work, if he really felt her mother's presence was a problem. Or he could take his blinders off and see that a dose of Emily Carson was better than most medicines.

"So…when are you going to tell Dad?"

Her mother glanced up, surprised. "I'm not."

"But—"

"I don't plan to tell him, Belle. And I'm going to ask you not to, either."

"I won't. But wouldn't it be better to get it out in the open before he just…finds out?"

"How would he find out?" Her mother's laugh had an edge. "He has no idea what I do all day, and even less interest. Oh, look…the sale section!"

Belle followed slowly. She couldn't quite understand this. How could her mother be so resolute, even courageous, about the need to do right by Adam, and so craven about telling her husband the truth?

"What if someone else tells him?"

"Who?" Two seconds after arriving at the fifty-percent-off rack, her mother had already found a fabulous violet silk sundress. She pulled it out triumphantly. "Ah! This is it!"

Belle ignored the diversion, though it was a gorgeous dress.

"I don't *know* who would tell him. It's always the person you least expect." Belle smiled, trying to soften her tone. "Remember the day Sue and I sneaked into the R-rated movie? Who could have guessed that Mrs.

Wickham's daughter's boyfriend would be selling popcorn? Believe me, someone always tells."

Her mother sobered. She folded her arms around the sundress. "You were thirteen, Belle. You were doing the wrong thing. What I'm doing is right."

"But that doesn't mean you won't get caught."

"It means that if I get caught, I'll deal with it. I won't be ashamed of what I've done. But I don't see any reason to invite trouble. Chances are your father will never find out. I'm not exactly going to camp out at Adam's bedside. I'm not sure when, or even if, I'll go again."

Belle felt oddly checkmated. Her mother's argument didn't really make sense, but she wasn't sure how to break into it. Perhaps, she thought as her mother held the violet dress out with a smile, the problem was that Belle wasn't asking the right questions.

She took the dress. She looked at the price tag before she let herself fall in love with its soft, liquid fabric and its elegant cut. With relief, she saw that she could afford it.

She held the dress up against her breast. "Like it?"

"It's marvelous." Her mother's eyes sparkled strangely. "You'll make a great success of this job, Belle. I know you will. I just don't—" with effort, she blinked away the mistiness "—I just don't quite remember when you stopped being my little girl."

"Mom." Belle had a sudden vision of the house she'd grown up in, with her mother and father living in it, like two ghosts who weren't really aware of one another. As if they lived in the same space, but in alternate universes. The isolation, especially for her mother, who craved intimacy more than her father ever had, must be almost unbearable.

"Mom," Belle said again urgently. "I know you don't like confrontation. But don't you ever just want to be honest with him? Don't you ever just want him to understand how you feel?"

Emily looked at her a minute and then slowly smiled. It was, Belle thought, the saddest smile she'd ever seen.

"No," she said. "Not anymore. I know you still want to be understood. Whether you like to admit it or not, you still want to fight your way to a real relationship with him. But all I want…"

She shrugged and turned back to the racks of clothes.

"All I want is peace."

SATURDAY MORNING AT THE Ferry Plaza Farmers Market was the most beautiful kind of insanity, with hundreds of people thronging through row upon row of gorgeous flowers, artistically arranged food and elegant wines. Belle and David used to come here every weekend, and they'd sit for a couple of hours drinking coffee, eating fresh-baked fruit Danishes from their favorite vendor, and watching the wind ruffle the bay.

Toward the end, when David began pushing for commitment, and tensions had run high, he'd begged off, saying he had briefs to write, or precedents to research. She'd continued coming alone, and had been strangely saddened to realize she didn't miss him at all. It was much more peaceful to read the paper in silence, without knowing he was on the other side of the table, watching her with those sad eyes, wondering why she didn't love him.

Since the breakup, she often wondered whether she'd run into him here, but she never had.

Until today.

She'd just claimed the only empty table, her coffee and pastry still precariously balanced on top of her *Chronicle,* when she saw him coming toward her, the collar of his windbreaker turned up, and the breeze romantically tousling his blond hair, as if he were arriving at a *GQ* photo shoot.

She forgot how handsome he was. The first time she'd met him, she'd assumed he must be one of the alpha bastards she'd sworn to avoid. But then she'd discovered the brains, the decency, the humility, beneath the looks. David Gerard was that romantic miracle, a beta-sweet boy-next-door who just happened to be movie-star gorgeous.

And she'd refused to marry him.

Maybe her father was right. Maybe she needed to have her head examined.

Belle wasn't sure how to handle this. It couldn't be a coincidence. He'd obviously come here specifically to see her. She arranged her things on the table, but remained standing, waiting for him to reach her.

As he drew closer, she could see that he looked somber, slightly awkward. Her mind darted through the possibilities. When he'd offered her the ring, he had sworn that, if she refused it, he would never ask her again. She had believed him. He wasn't here to beg for another chance.

Besides, this meeting seemed carefully chosen to provide face-to-face time without true intimacy. He'd opted out of the more impersonal phone call, as well as the more dangerous knock on the apartment door.

"Hi," she said, for want of anything else to say. She smiled, because she really did like him very much and was glad to see him, in spite of everything. She had been heartsick when she finally had to face the fact she couldn't turn all this admiration and affection into love.

"Hi." He looked as if he wasn't sure whether they should shake hands, hug…or what. Finally he just gestured to the other chair. "Is it okay if I sit down for a minute? I'd like to talk to you about something."

"Of course." She edged her newspaper out of the way, so that his spot was clear. Then she sat, motioning for him to do the same. "Want to split the Danish? I shouldn't eat the whole thing, anyhow."

"No, thanks. I'm not hungry."

She nodded, wishing she could help him relax. That last day, she had told him she hoped they could go back to being friends, but he'd just laughed. That laugh had been the most brittle sound.

Clearly, judging from the tension in his voice and posture, he still wasn't ready for friendship.

"It's warm, isn't it?" She took off her sweater and bunched it up on the tabletop. She leaned back in the chair and turned her face up to the nearly cloudless blue sky. "It's heavenly. We don't get many days like this."

"No. No, we don't." David cleared his throat. "Look, Belle. I hear you went to work for Diamante Pizza."

She sat straight again. So much for neutral chit-chat. "Yes."

He toyed with the edge of her newspaper, folding

down the corner, then opening it up again. "I'm sorry. I know that must have been a tough decision to make."

"Yes. It was hard, at first. But…" She hesitated.

"But what?" His fingers paused on the newspaper. "Don't tell me you *like* it."

Something in his tone irritated her, though she knew that wasn't fair. He was only reacting to what she'd always told him—that public relations was a snake pit she hoped to God she'd never fall into.

But so far, her job hadn't been anything like the hypocritical, back-slapping, good-old-boy hellhole she'd imagined. So far, work at Diamante had been honest, creative, strategic and fun.

Of course, tonight she would attend her first major social event, a fund-raiser at the Moorehead Museum, an organization Diamante sponsored heavily. Tonight, when drinks and power were flowing, and everyone was busy trying to keep it flowing in their own direction, she might see a different side of things.

"I wouldn't say I like it. But maybe my attitude before was a little extreme. You know, the kind of blind prejudice that is really ignorance in disguise. The Malones are businessmen and pizza makers. They don't have time to sort out the intricacies of the press. What's wrong with hiring professional communicators to help them communicate better?"

For a minute he just looked at her. Then he shook his head. "I never thought I'd hear you say that."

"I know." She smiled. "It surprises the heck out of me, too. But surely it's okay to learn new things. To open your eyes? To broaden your outlook?"

He shrugged. "As long as *broadening* isn't brain-washing in disguise."

"It's not."

"Okay." He shifted his gaze to the bay, which glittered like a piece of sequined gray silk under the summer sunlight. "But…I do hear Matt Malone is quite charming."

She had been trying not to get defensive, but this was too much. It had been bad enough for David to hint that she might have been a sucker, falling hard for the PR department's in-house hype. Was he now accusing her of selling out her principles to the sexiest bidder?

Did he really believe that, or was this just emotional payback?

"David," she said, turning to face him squarely. "You didn't come all the way out here just to talk to me about Diamante Pizza, did you?"

"Yes," he said calmly. "Actually, I did."

She subsided, too surprised to have a ready comeback. "Oh," was the best she could do. "Why?"

"I have a client who used to work for them."

She waited. David had two kinds of clients. The very, very rich who wanted to protect their business assets, and the very, very poor who had been abused by their employers and needed free representation. But they both deserved confidentiality, and got it. It was rare to hear him mention a client at all.

"I can't tell you his name, but he's given me permission to talk to you about his brief. The bottom line is, he wants to sue Diamante."

"For what?"

"Apparently they have a charity fund, to be disbursed to employees who are facing personal emergencies. They call it the Drivers Fund. Have you heard of it?"

"Yes. No detail, though. Just its existence." Since it didn't intersect with her duties, she hadn't ever really paid attention. She only knew that Todd Kirkland administered it from a nice window office at the far end of the corporate building.

"Well, my client, who was turned down when he applied for assistance, believes that the money is being mishandled."

"By whom?"

"My client suspects that a Todd Kirkland must be acting on behalf of or at least in collaboration with Matt Malone. Apparently it's a great deal of money, most of it contributed by the company and therefore tax deductible, but also quite a bit coming from the paychecks of the employees."

Belle could confirm that. Human Resources had explained it to her in general terms during her orientation. Liking the concept, she'd gladly signed the little box that donated an hour of wages per pay period.

"It's supposed to go to the needy employees." David scratched his cheek as he always did when he was deeply interested in a case. "But my client's feeling is that it's more or less a slush fund for the management."

The rush of instinctive resistance that flooded her was a shock. She had been with Diamante Pizza only two weeks now. Why should she feel personally assaulted by this allegation?

And why should she be so sure it couldn't be true?

"I hope your client has more than 'feelings' if you're planning to bring this to a lawsuit. That kind of publicity can seriously damage a company's reputation."

"God, Belle." David frowned. "Can you hear yourself? You already sound like a PR person. I'm telling you this because I think you might be able to help me."

She shifted her pastry on its paper plate. "How?"

"You're on scene. You know these people, and you know the setup. You're a damn talented investigative journalist. I want you to investigate. Find out whether there's anything to it."

She took a deep breath, inhaling the mix of food scents and sea salt that was the Ferry Building. Suddenly, it just smelled confused and mildly dirty.

"You want me to spy on the company I work for?"

"I want you to look for the facts. If the little guys are getting screwed here, I want you to help me prove that. This is the kind of exposé you used to drool over, remember?"

"Of course, but—"

"But if the company is clean, if my guy is wrong, maybe the facts you find can make him see reason. Maybe we can talk him out of…what did you call it? Damaging Diamante's reputation?"

David was intense. Not angry—he rarely got angry about anything. But hyperfocused, like a dog gnawing a bone. He never took his eyes off Belle's face.

She looked away, needing a respite from that piercing gaze. A curvaceous street performer was walking by, covered completely in silver paint, wearing silver clothes, even silver sneakers and gloves. Everyone around them was staring at the woman, who was clearly intrigued by David.

As she came abreast, she tossed him a white-toothed smile that looked eerie in her silver face.

But he didn't even seem to notice.

Belle had always liked that about him. He had eyes only for her. But right now that gaze was too probing, too disapproving.

"Well?" He still watched her. "What do you say?"

"I don't know." She took a bite of Danish, though it was cold now, and she was no longer hungry. She wiped strawberry from the corner of her lips. "Heck, I don't even know that I *could* dig up anything relevant. I'm the newbie, remember? They have me essentially sharpening pencils so far. I don't have the secret codes to the lockbox or anything."

"I'm not talking about creeping around Malone's office with a camera you hide in your lip gloss." He shook his head. "Come on, Belle. This is what you do. What you *used* to do. And you're good at it. Remember the story you did on the councilman who let the lobbyists remodel his beach house for nearly nothing? You uncovered that with public records and phone calls. With analytical skills and common sense."

She felt a small melting sensation in her chest. Yes, she had been good at that. And she had loved it.

"But...don't you have real investigators you can hire this out to?"

"That would take money. This guy isn't able to pay me, much less a P.I."

As if he could sense that she was wavering, David

leaned back in his chair with a sigh. He lowered his chin and gave her the look that had shamed a hundred juries into finding for his clients.

"I'm asking for a favor here. Just one favor. It's not illegal, unethical or wrong in any way. Don't you owe me that much?"

For breaking up with him, he meant. Didn't she owe him one favor, in return for the way she'd handed his diamond ring back to him, stamped Rejected, and garnished with little slivers of his heart?

For the first time since the conversation had begun, she wondered whether he might have brought this idea to her merely so that he'd have an excuse to see her again.

It didn't really matter, though. Whatever his reason for extending the bait, she'd bitten. Hard. She was hooked.

"I can't promise anything," she said, already mulling over which databases she'd search first. "But I'll...I'll look into it."

CHAPTER SEVEN

BELLE WAS A LITTLE late to the party. She'd been ready
an hour early, right down to the contacts she'd chosen
instead of her glasses. But at the last minute she'd
decided her dress wasn't right, and knocked on Pandora's door, hoping to borrow something fantastic.

She recognized the irony. The last time she'd attended a party where she would see Matt Malone, she'd
allowed Pandora to choose her outfit. And look how that
had turned out.

This time, she insisted on pure professionalism, even
though Pandora, who always thought in terms of
dramatic effect, decided that this would be the perfect
occasion to remind Matt Malone where he had met his
new PR employee before.

"Come on, let's do it," she'd said, laughing and
holding out her belly-dancing bra and skirt, which was
similar enough to the old Cleopatra costume to ring a
bell in even the dullest brain. "Let's see if he was ham-
mered completely blind that night or not."

"No." Belle had strong-armed the gauzy material
away and made herself at home in Pandora's closet.
She flicked through the velvets, sequined-satins and

purple poodle skirts. "Don't you have anything sensible? No wonder you can't ever persuade anyone to give you a loan."

Pandora laughed. "I got a loan just today, thank you very much," she said, sniffing indignantly. "Well, not a loan, but more like a…donation."

She looked dreamy-eyed for a minute, and Belle wondered whether there was a new guy in the picture. The last time she'd seen Pandora look like that, the result, nine months later, had been little Mary Isabella.

Pandora seemed to pull herself together with a toss of her dark hair. "But that's a story for another day. I'm serious, Belle. Why don't we just drag this silly skeleton out of the closet? Tell him. What's the big deal? He's not going to fire you because once upon a time you kissed him in the starlight."

Belle had refused to be drawn in, and eventually Pandora had produced a fabulous steel-blue cocktail dress with a ballerina neckline and a sprinkling of sequins. It fit almost perfectly, though ordinarily Pandora's clothes had an extra inch or two in the bust. Pandora had the world's sexiest collection of shoes, so she added strappy silver sandals with heels so high Belle prayed she wouldn't have to handle stairs.

But at least when she arrived at the museum's Patrons Room, which sparkled with crystal flutes, gold-filtered accent lighting and sterling silver trays floating around on the gloved hands of white-coated waiters, she fit in with the rest of the self-assured professionals.

She'd covered a couple of these elegant events in her short stint as a reporter, so she knew that the guests would be spread out in half a dozen areas—here by the bar, the dance floor in the old planetarium space, the buffet area off in an octagonal side room, and even the courtyard, where a mini-botanical garden was a lovely excuse to steal a private flirtation. It would be possible to stay at the party all night and not see everyone.

Still, naively, she searched the place, looking for Matt. George must have been waiting for her, because within sixty seconds he came rushing over, bringing a middle-aged man by the arm.

"Andy, I'd like you to meet my new assistant, Belle Carson. The Cinnamon Diamond Treasure Hunt was her idea. Belle, Andy Carlito makes the boxes Diamante pizzas are delivered in. Cinnamon Diamonds, too, starting next month."

The man shook her hand with an enthusiasm that was obviously genuine. "I love the idea," he said. "Women hunting for diamond rings in their sweets. It's perfect. Matt will sell a million of these to hopeful females, and everyone will need a box!" He laughed. "The pastries, that is. Not the women."

She laughed, ridiculously pleased by his approval. He was fat, red-faced and fifty, but the look in his eye was intelligent. And he wasn't a chauvinist. He noticed her dress, of course—it was a wonderful dress—but the real spark in his eyes had been lit by her idea.

They talked awhile, and then George excused them both so that he could, as he put it, show her off to everyone else. By the time she'd been introduced to half a dozen of Diamante's most important associates, they'd made their way into the round, dome-ceilinged ballroom.

And she had overcome most of her jitters.

PR wasn't so hard. She could do this.

"I know you must be breaking me in easy," she said under her breath in one of the few moments when she and George were alone. "These people are all allies. When do I get to meet an enemy or two?"

George laughed. "Diamante doesn't have enemies, Belle."

She thought of David's client and his accusations. "Everyone has enemies."

George didn't seem to be listening. He was in full-throttle PR gear, scanning the room continuously, checking to see where he might be needed.

Suddenly she felt his hand tighten on her elbow.

"Okay, you want something tough? How about Matt's brothers and grandmother? Redmond and Colby Malone, flanking Angelina. Just off to your right, at eleven-thirty."

She kept a neutral smile on her face as she glanced smoothly to her right. But her mouth went dry.

Colby and Red Malone. Tall, graceful, smiling. Dark-haired, like Matt, but with fair skin instead of the olive-gold complexion that made their brother so exotic.

Still…clearly related, clearly endowed with the same incredible sex appeal. And between them stood a slim, elegantly upright woman with a cloud of white hair and delicate, olive-toned features that would forever label her a beauty.

A daunting trio. But it was Colby who made Belle's heart tighten uncomfortably. She definitely remembered him. He'd been the brother standing in the ballroom eight years ago, the one Matt had checked with before leaving. The one who had eyed her coolly, then whispered something to Matt about the dangers of driving drunk.

Colby Malone hadn't been plastered that night. Suddenly Belle wasn't willing to take the chance that he might recognize her.

"No," she said quietly but urgently. "Not quite ready for that gauntlet, I'm afraid. Got anything less daunting?"

George chuckled sympathetically. "Don't blame you. An audience with the queen isn't an entry-level assignment. Let's see…how about—" He smiled. "Oh, perfect timing. Here comes Matt. He must have marching orders for us."

That was when Belle realized what a fool she really was. *Marching orders.* That was why Matt would seek them out. Not to socialize, not to tell her how pretty her dress was. To deploy them on some public relations mission.

And why shouldn't he? She and George were his employees. His hired joy machines, paid to rotate around the room like robots, strategically spraying smiles and compliments wherever they would bear the most fruit.

Had she let herself forget that, even for a split second? Had some weak, ridiculous part of her mind imagined that she was dressing up for a date?

She watched, feeling her smile go stiff and numb on her face, as Matt stopped to kiss his grandmother and whisper something in her ear.

Angelina tilted her head and gave him a glance that was equal parts affection and exasperation. Then Colby intervened, sweeping Angelina into his arms and whisking her onto the dance floor.

The woman danced as if she were twenty. She floated by, catching Belle's gaze for a split second with her intelligent, twinkling eyes. Belle's mouth went dry.

Yesterday afternoon, before breaking for the weekend, Belle had written a draft of a speech for Mrs. Malone to deliver at the product launch press conference.

She wondered uncomfortably if it was too late to get the draft back. If only she'd met the woman before she wrote it. The words had been crafted with an older, softer, more matronly grandmother in mind.

The speech she'd written was too cute, Belle recognized with growing dissatisfaction. Too cliché. This sharp-eyed, regal matriarch would hate it.

God, would Belle never stop overestimating herself—and underestimating this job? She had been so smug just five minutes ago. Now she saw that she wasn't through screwing up. Not by a long shot.

"Hey, George," Matt said as he finally made it to their little corner. He shook his hand, then turned to Belle with a smile. "Has George been introducing you to everyone you need to meet?"

"Yes," she said, refusing to be disappointed that he hadn't complimented the dress. How perverse would that be? She knew darn well that if he had, she would have thought him sexist. After all, he looked terrific in that tuxedo, but she wasn't likely to tell him so.

There were rules about that in the workplace, anyhow.

"George has been very conscientious. I've met at least a hundred people in the past hour alone."

George nodded. "I got her face time with most of the suppliers, and a couple of the TV types. I haven't seen many of the government group here yet, but we'll hit those when they arrive."

"Fine. Anyone you need me to set up for you?"

George let his gaze circle the room once. "No, I think I can handle most of this crowd, but check with me when the second wave comes through, just in case?" George let his gaze circle the room once. "Belle's met half the room already. She's made quite a splash."

"I don't doubt it for a minute," Matt said, and his smile was warm enough to give her a slight sizzle.

He didn't overdo it, though, almost immediately turning back to George. "I've just heard that Overholzer is going to be filming at Flint Park next week. A couple of big name stars, according to the rumors. The blonde...you know the one? Anyhow, they've already got catering lined up, of course, but I was wondering if we could make some friendly, neighborhood gesture. You know, get a pizza or two in there somehow."

"Absolutely." George looked excited. "Local TV will be all over it. Yeah, we need that Diamante box in the background. Cinnamon Diamonds, too. Can't beat that for product placement."

"Ken Castle is the one who told me about it. He's outside with Mayor Rhoeban. See what you can find out, okay?" Matt touched Belle's shoulder. "I've got a few people I'd like to introduce Belle to, anyhow."

Oh, no, no...

His fingers felt cool, and the skin between her shoulder blades began to prickle. She didn't want to be alone with him, not when she was all dressed up in borrowed sequins, and he was looking like every woman's sweetest dream in that tuxedo.

"You don't think I should go with George?" She was glad she didn't sound as tense as she felt. "I haven't met Mayor Rhoeban, and—"

"No, he's not important." Matt's cheek dimpled subtly. "Though, just for the record, I never said that."

George was already gone, anyhow. She looked at the back of his departing tuxedo with a sinking heart. She resisted the urge to fiddle with the curls she knew had started to spring out of their careful upsweep. She had very determined hair, and bobbie pins and styling mousse could only do so much.

Finally, taking a deep breath, she turned back and faced Matt.

He was staring at her, his head tilted in that way she found so impossibly endearing. She squared her shoulders, determined not to melt.

"You don't look very happy, Belle. Aren't you having any fun tonight?"

She smiled politely, ignoring how sexy her name sounded on his lips. Ignoring the fact that he shouldn't care whether she was happy.

"I'm learning a lot," she said carefully. "That's what I'm here for. I'm here to do the best job I can representing Diamante."

"Yes," he said. "But that's easier to do if you're also having fun."

He didn't wait for a response, which was lucky, because she didn't have one.

Instead, to her surprise he simply extended a hand. "I'll tell you how you can really make Diamante Pizza look good. Let the company CEO be seen dancing with the prettiest woman in the room."

She stared at his hand. She knew how it would feel, sliding around her waist. She knew, as if it had happened to her yesterday instead of eight years ago. It was a tactile memory that held ten times the power of sight or sound.

But what if it held the same power for him?

What if, when she drifted into his arms, he remembered?

Maybe Pandora was right. Maybe it didn't really matter. He was a man of the world, and he'd danced with a thousand women. Kissed a hundred. And done more than that with most of them.

Far more than he'd ever done with her.

If he remembered, they'd probably just have a mutual laugh about it. He'd think back, remembering the wig and the lipstick, the jingling gold coins and the absurdly padded bra. He'd mock himself for passing out. It would become their joke. The office joke, perhaps.

"Oh, I'm sorry," she said, thinking as fast as she could. "But I'm really a terrible dancer. Just awful. Believe me, it will only destroy your reputation to be seen out there with me."

He raised one eyebrow. "Somehow I can't believe that—"

He broke off as someone jostled him roughly from behind. He had to step toward her, just to keep his balance. At first she thought it was one of the dancers.

Though they were standing safely in an alcove, the band had begun playing a fast song, and the floor was getting crowded.

"Matt, there you are."

It wasn't a dancer. It was Todd Kirkland. Belle would have known he was drunk from the unfocused glaze in his eye, even if she hadn't smelled the liquor emanating from his body. He smelled of liquor the way she had smelled of coffee on her first morning at work.

Except she was pretty sure he hadn't spilled it. Every drop had made its way down his throat, and from there straight to his brain. He could hardly remain upright. His feet were stationary, but his upper body was weaving slightly, like a buoy at sea.

His eyes were red, damp in the creases.

"Matt, Matt, son, I've been looking for you."

"And you found me. It's okay, Todd. I'm here." Matt put his hand on the older man's shoulder, either to reassure him or to keep him from falling over. Then he tossed Belle a tight smile over his shoulder. "See if you can find George?"

She nodded, turning immediately, trying to remember the quickest way to the courtyard. She knew it would be a public-relations nightmare if Todd Kirkland made a conspicuous scene.

It would be bad enough for any employee to drink himself into a weeping fit in the middle of a party full of power brokers and members of the press. For Todd to do it would be lethal. He held a position of authority and trust. He controlled a large sum of...

She came to a dead stop, halfway between the dance

floor and the buffet table, and forced herself to finish
the thought.

Todd Kirkland controlled a large sum of money.

Two hours later, long after Todd and Matt had left, with
the rest of the Malones following almost immediately
after, Belle was dancing. Her partner was Brian Drayson,
an old friend from the *Chronicle,* a business reporter who
was clearly hoping she'd spill some dirt on Diamante.

She knew what he wanted, of course. In his shoes,
she would have done the same thing. Diamante had a
squeaky-clean reputation, something that always made
business reporters suspicious.

Belle had researched the company thoroughly herself, equally suspicious, before she reported for her first
day, and she knew the folklore surrounding it. Colm and
Angelina Malone, the son of an Irish immigrant and the
daughter of an Italian physician, had married young
and lived poor while Colm attended business school.
Angelina baked cookies for extra income, but her specialty was pizza.

When Colm graduated, he worked for another restaurant chain for years before he decided he wanted his
kitchen. So he'd opened Diamante Pizza. They worked
side by side for twenty years, Angelina in the kitchen
and Colm managing the money, refusing to expand,
refusing to let greed separate them.

Finally, when their son grew up, married and started
having boys of his own, Colm agreed to branch out,
opening the franchises that delivered the now-famous
Diamante pizza. Then tragedy struck. The son and his

wife had died in an accident nearly fifteen years ago, leaving all three boys in the care of Colm and Angelina.

And now one of those grandsons, the middle one, Matt, had picked up the torch. He would carry on the family tradition, and even expand it.

It sounded too ideal to be true. That's what set Brian's investigative reporter antennae quivering.

But Belle didn't mind being used a little. She loved to dance, and Brian was much better at that than he was at extracting information. Besides, she was using him, too. She was letting him brag about his investigatory acumen, all the while filing away ideas that would help as she looked into the secrets of Todd Kirkland and the Diamante Drivers Fund.

He'd just mentioned an interesting Web site that tracked certain public documents, and she was repeating the URL in her head, committing it to memory, when she looked up and saw…

It couldn't be! He had left hours ago….

But it was. Matt Malone stood in the doorway of the ballroom, talking affably to a young man with a huge nose and a cartoon cowlick. Belle's mind raced, but went nowhere. She stared at her boss with the helpless fatalism of a deer about to be felled by a semi, which meant she saw exactly what happened to his expression when he noticed her.

The chill of it reached all the way across the ballroom and made her shiver. Her feet slowed, then stopped.

Brian leaned back to get a look at her. "What's wrong?"

"I'm sorry," she said, giving him an apologetic touch on the forearm. "I need to talk to my boss for a minute."

Brian glanced over and saw Matt. "Oh, excellent. I thought he was gone. Introduce me?"

"Later." She had no idea what she was going to say, but she had to say something.

He watched her coming toward him, but made no effort to meet her halfway. He merely kept talking to the cowlick man, winding that up with a handshake and a smile just as she arrived.

"I'm sorry," she said after the man walked away, though she didn't specify sorry for what. "I didn't realize you were still here. Is Todd okay?"

"He's fine, thanks."

She couldn't tell if he was annoyed or just tired…or whether she might even be imagining that there was anything odd in his manner at all. Maybe it was just her conscience playing tricks on her. She felt guilty, embarrassed at being caught in a lie, but perhaps he didn't even remember that she'd said she was a terrible dancer.

His expression was harder to read, up close.

She bit her lower lip. "Is there anything I can do?"

"Not tonight." He gave her a long, assessing look. "But you'll need to come in early on Monday. I'm afraid the speech you wrote for my grandmother won't work. I've sent comments to George, and he'll go over them with you in the morning. I need a revised version by noon."

Belle was used to being edited, and she wasn't sensitive about her work. But his tone was so dismissive, as if he'd expected her work to be subpar, and she hadn't let him down. It stung. Her writing talent was practically the only skill she'd brought to the job, and apparently he didn't think that was worth much, either.

"I'm sorry it wasn't on target," she said. "I'll be there early, and I'll make it right. I think you'll find I'm a quick study."

"Of course you are." He smiled coolly. "Just look how quickly you picked up dancing."

Her face flamed. "I'm sorry about that—it's just that I—"

"No need to explain," he said. "You should dance whenever you want. And you should decline to dance whenever it suits you. I have no problem with that."

"But—"

"What I do have a problem with," he went on, as if she hadn't spoken, "is disloyalty."

Her throat felt frozen. Was it possible he'd already learned that she was looking into the Drivers Fund for David? How could he have heard? No one knew…

"Disloyalty?"

"That's right. Make up your mind about what you want, Belle. Because Diamante is my family business, my grandmother's life's work. It won't be a temporary lily pad for an out-of-work journalist. I won't tolerate an employee using my time, and my contacts, to try to dance her way back into the newspaper business."

CHAPTER EIGHT

THE SUNDAY AFTERNOON sky was sponged white with clouds, and the ocean was more choppy than curled, so for surfing the day had been more or less a bust.

But for rest and relaxation, which Matt needed desperately, it had been perfect.

A couple of hours ago, Matt and Colby had given up on finding a decent wave. They propped their boards up, nose deep in the sand, then just sat on their low-slung beach chairs and surrendered to the pleasures of drinking cool beer and admiring hot bikinis.

"Oh, yeah," Colby said with a sigh, as a pair of perfect tens went jogging by, bare feet splashing in the water's edge. "I definitely needed a day off."

Matt agreed wholeheartedly, but he was too lethargic to form words. His skin had that warm, tight feeling that came from drying salt, and he was starting to get a nice buzz from the beer.

That was the advantage of practically never drinking. Didn't take much to get you into the zone.

Colby looked up at the sun, then down at his watch.

"Last call," he said merrily, and pulled the final two bottles from the cooler, which, as always, had held only six to start with.

It was a tradition none of them ever questioned, though they'd begun it so long ago they'd nearly forgotten where it came from. When their parents died in a train wreck on a European trip, Colby had been eighteen, Matt sixteen and Red only fifteen. They'd been staying with Nana Lina and Grandpa Colm, and after the tragedy, they just never went home.

It had been indescribably hard, but they'd survived, mostly because their grandparents were such amazing people.

Angelina and Colm Malone were strict, with almost impossibly high standards for their grandsons, but unconditional love flowed from them like water from a gushing spring. The boys learned right away that they could never forfeit the love, but respect would be a prize they had to earn.

That first summer, Grandpa Colm had sat them down and talked about the liquor rules. Never mind that none of them was legally old enough to drink. Years before they ever tasted beer, they solemnly promised, right there in Nana Lina's living room, that their official limit would always be one six-pack a day, divided two ways or three, depending on how many brothers had come along. They would never touch toe to water once they'd begun to drink. And they would stop two hours before they left the beach.

It was a promise they'd rarely been tempted to break.

So far today, Matt had drunk two. Colby bumped the third against Matt's knee, offering it up, but he shook his head.

"Hey, you never told me what happened last night," Colby said as he unscrewed the top of his own beer. He took a long swig. "With Todd, I mean. He looked wrecked."

"He was." Matt closed his eyes against the sun, which had come out from behind the clouds, setting the tips of the waves on fire. "I got him home. He's probably still sleeping it off."

Colby was quiet a minute, and Matt knew his big brother was trying to decide whether to pursue this. Matt sent out *don't go there* vibes, but apparently he was too sleepy to be effective, because in a few seconds Colby cleared his throat.

"Guess that settles the question, then," his brother said, his voice artificially neutral. "The question about whether he's drinking too much."

Damn it. Matt didn't want to think about this right now. He'd just barely managed to forget last night and all its exasperating moments.

But it was inevitable that Colby was going to want to hash this out. Matt had hired Todd Kirkland five years ago, against the objections of everyone except Nana Lina. Colby and Red had always thought Todd was exploiting Matt, playing on his sympathies.

And maybe he was. Todd's son, Doug, had been a college friend of Matt's. He'd died his senior year, of a sudden pneumonia that took hold before anyone realized how sick he was. Todd had fallen apart, started drinking, lost his job and nearly lost his marriage.

When Todd finally pulled himself up and made a new start five years ago, he'd come to Matt for a job, and Matt hadn't had the heart to turn him down.

He hadn't regretted that moment of sympathy. Until

last night, Todd had been the perfect employee, gradually taking on more responsibility as time passed, the tragedy receded and he grew stronger.

"I wouldn't judge him too harshly based on last night," Matt said, adjusting his sunglasses to block the glittering waves. "Yesterday was a tough day for Todd. I'd forgotten, but apparently it would have been Doug's thirtieth birthday. It just got to him, that's all."

"Okay. We can cut him some slack for last night." Colby planted his beer in the sand beside him. "But if he starts drinking like that on a regular basis, you're going to have problems, Matt. I'm talking as your lawyer here. I know you feel sorry for the guy. But you need to protect yourself. You need to protect the company."

Matt nodded slowly. "I will. But I'm not going to fire the man because he had a few too many on his dead son's birthday. I talked to Nana Lina about it, and she agrees. We're going to let it go this time."

"God. What a couple of softies. Under that shark's exterior, Nana Lina is as big a marshmallow as you are."

"You'd better not let her hear you say it."

"Hell, no, and if you tell her, I'll…" Colby laughed. "I'll call Tiffani and explain how much you miss her."

Matt groaned. "Don't even joke about that. The woman already calls twice a week, just to see if I've changed my mind. I'm thinking about introducing her to Stony."

"Oh. That bad, huh?"

Colby knew that bringing out Stony Jones was like rolling out the big cannons. Stony Jones was a professional surfer, a Yale business school grad who, like Matt, had discovered a serious aversion to office work. He had ditched all that and built his surfing talent and handsome face into a lucrative franchise. He pitched everything from surfboards to sunscreen.

Occasionally, when Matt needed a graceful way out of a souring relationship, he'd arrange for Stony to saunter in and save the day. Women couldn't resist Stony's mesmerizing mixture of bad boy beach bum and gilded sun god.

Stony didn't mind, as long as the castoffs were gorgeous. He went through women like bags of hard candy anyhow, so everyone came out a winner. Especially Matt. When the Stony-struck women broke up with him, they were always touched by how mature and forgiving he could be.

Matt nodded. "She's definitely that bad. I blame her parents. They should have told her no once or twice along the way. It might not be such a shock now."

"Okay, so you let Stony fix the problem. What then? Want me to introduce you to Stephanie's friend Cindi Sullivan?"

"Maybe. No. I don't know." He raised his sunglasses briefly and glanced at his brother. "Is that Cindi with an *i?*"

Colby laughed. "Of course."

Matt lowered his glasses again. "Then no."

"What? A woman's got to have some intellectual name now, like Hildegarde or Mildred, before you'll give her the time of day?"

Matt shut his eyes. "I don't have the time of day to give to anyone. To tell you the truth, I'd just about decided to take a break for a while, but—"

"Take a break from *women?*"

Colby's shock was almost comical. Particularly because Matt knew that, of all the Malone brothers, Colby actually cared the least about his romances. His heart had been broken years ago, and while it had apparently healed, it hadn't ever worked quite right again.

"Yes, from women." Matt shook his head. "It's possible."

"Yeah, but is it *healthy?*"

Two days ago, Matt could have answered that without thinking. But after last night...

"I don't know," he admitted. "I'm not sure anymore. Something's wrong with me. At the party last night, I made a damn fool of myself with a woman from work."

"A woman from work? Hell, Matt, how stupid can you—" He broke off, openmouthed. "Oh, my God. You don't mean you and Francie—"

Matt laughed out loud. "God, no. Not Francie. I said I'd been dumb, not insane. It was George's new hire. In the PR department. I don't think you've met her yet. Her name is Belle Carson. A blonde?"

"Right. I saw her with George last night." Colby frowned. "Cute curls, innocent eyes, serious, heart-shaped face? All she needs is the little red hood to finish the picture."

It wasn't a bad description, actually, at least on the surface. Matt fought the urge to explain that it took a while to spot the flash of intelligence in Belle's wide blue eyes, or the stubborn spunk that could set that delicate jaw in a formidable thrust.

"That's the one." He smiled. "She's not as helpless as she looks."

"Maybe not. But she's not your type. She's under-stated. Refined. She's somebody's trophy-wife-to-be."

Matt scooped a cool spot into the sand with his heels and tried to get comfortable. He was getting seriously annoyed, and he didn't want to let it get out of control.

"Maybe you don't know as much about my type as you think you do."

"Well, I've observed that you like them with a little more…shall we say, air in the tires?" Colby chuckled. "This lady is two kids and yoga classes. She's healthy dinners, an hour of TV and five minutes in the mission-ary position. Unless she has a headache."

At that, Matt's temper flared to life.

"Hell, Colby, that's about the most superficial crap you've ever spouted. Let's just overlook the real truth, which is that if Haley Watson had been willing to give you a *lifetime* of the missionary position, you'd have jumped at the chance. But beyond that, what the hell do you really know about Belle Carson?"

His brother didn't answer immediately. The air was heavy between them, as if the sunny day suddenly threatened rain. Matt had gone too far. None of them ever, ever mentioned Haley Watson—not to Colby, and not even to each other. He thought about apologizing, but that would just make it worse.

Finally, Colby set his empty beer can into the cooler and leaned forward, his elbows on his knees.

"I don't know anything about her," he said, and his tone carried enough humility to double as an apology.

"Except she must be pretty amazing, to get you this worked up."

Matt shrugged, which was his version of accepting the apology. "She's not amazing. She's just…interesting." He smiled at his brother ruefully. "And for some reason I can't understand, every time I look at her, I want to tear her clothes off."

Colby took off his sunglasses and let them dangle from one finger. "How far did it go? Did you sleep with her?"

"Hell, no. She works for me, remember? I can't touch her. I can't even look at her longer than three-point-two seconds."

"Correct," Colby said, obviously relieved. "And don't you ever forget it."

"I won't. But it's making me nuts. And last night, it made me worse than nuts. It made me mean. I saw her dancing with some moron from the *Chronicle,* and I chewed her out about a bunch of stupid stuff at work, stuff that doesn't really matter at all."

"Nice," Colby observed. "Bet she really likes you now, Einstein."

"I'm sure she hates me. Which ought to simplify things, but unfortunately doesn't." He ran his hand over his face, wiping away any lingering grains of sand. "Man. What a mess."

Colby shook his head. "Yep. Okay, want your lawyer's opinion or your brother's opinion?"

"Let's start with the lawyer."

"Fire her while she's still in her ninety-day probation period. Wait a year or two, then arrange to bump into her somewhere and see if she wants to have dinner. The odds of scoring aren't great, but the odds of escaping a lawsuit are excellent."

Matt hated that idea. "And the brother's opinion?"

"You're just horny. Let me call Cindi Sullivan, whose bust-to-waist ratio is amazing. I'd be willing to bet little Belle won't look so interesting after a long, hot summer with Cindi."

Matt laughed. "That's all you've got?"

Colby stood and began folding up his chair. "Well, you could try to control yourself. No offense, but that one is the longest shot of all."

BY LATE SUNDAY AFTERNOON, Belle's eyes were bloodshot and bleary from staring at the computer screen all day.

She'd done searches on everything in Todd Kirkland's life that could conceivably be a matter of public record. She had learned that his wife worked for the school department as an administrative assistant. She had a list of every car he'd ever owned. She knew which neighbor had complained to the city about the height of his fence, and when the fence came down. She'd found out which year his mother's will had been probated. She saw the obituary notice that said his son had died in college. And she'd read the full sad story about the two businesses he'd incorporated, then declared bankruptcy on, during the years right after the tragedy.

No red flags, but a few that might be caution yellow.

For instance, ten years ago, presumably when things were the bleakest after the death of his son, he'd lost his house in foreclosure. He didn't buy another until five years ago, when he went to work for Diamante and purchased a modest place in Encino.

The odd development was that he'd sold the Encino house last year, without making much profit, and bought a new one worth three times as much. Belle could find nothing that indicated a legitimate influx of cash. No promotions at Diamante, no inheritances that she could track down, no lottery wins.

Obviously it meant nothing by itself, but it was curious. Something to check on.

Funny what a great motivator anger could be, she thought as she stretched her back, took off her glasses and rubbed her aching eyes. If Matt Malone hadn't been such an SOB at the party last night…

Her doorbell rang.

She closed out of the tax appraiser's Web site, slid her feet back into the sneakers she'd kicked off under the computer desk, popped her glasses back onto her nose, then opened the door.

She'd been half expecting Pandora, who sometimes needed a babysitter on Sunday afternoons, but the angry face at her door belonged to her father, instead.

"Hi, Dad," she said, surprised and a little uncomfortable. He rarely came to her apartment, which wasn't up to his standards. He preferred her to come to him. "Is everything okay?"

He looked over her shoulder into the tiny living room. "Any reason I can't come in?"

She smiled. "If you're asking whether there's a half-naked man in my bedroom, the answer is no." She started to add "unfortunately," but figured that wasn't necessarily the joke you wanted to share with your father.

Especially when he was already glowering like a thundercloud. He entered the apartment aggressively, but once he was in he looked oddly out of place and uncertain. Though she'd done her best to make the flat clean, colorful and welcoming, it was an old building, neither very elegant nor very large. The kitchen, dining area and living room together could all have fit into his study at home.

"Dad, what's up?"

"I don't know, Belle." He put his hands on his hips. "Maybe you should tell me."

When she felt the first squirm of anxiety, so familiar from her childhood, she clamped down on it hard. She knew this game. It was a bully's favorite. The hourglass of his temper ticked down while she tried to Guess Why Daddy's Mad.

Forget it. She was not going to play.

"Dad, I'm very tired. I've got the headache from hell. If you want something, you're just going to have to tell me what it is."

"I want to know where your mother is."

Damn it. Belle had no idea what the right answer was. She honestly didn't know whether her mother might be at the hospital visiting Adam, but she certainly didn't want to say the wrong thing.

"Why? Do you think there's been an accident or something?"

"Of course not. We had an argument. She's not answering her cell phone."

"So. She's mad, and she wants some time alone. Let her have it."

He waved that possibility off irritably, then glanced toward her bedroom. She had closed the door out of habit, thinking Pandora might bring Mary Isabella over. Babies and cluttered closets didn't mix.

He gave Belle a hard stare, the one he probably used at the dealership to terrify his employees. "Is she *here?*"

"Dad. Get serious. No."

He lowered his brows, then, without another word, turned on his heel and headed toward the bedroom door.

She thought about trying to stop him, but how absurd would that look? Lurching across her living room, throwing herself against the door? A tug-of-war with the knob?

Instead, she just called out, "Raoul, honey, put some clothes on. My dad's coming in."

Her father hesitated, just for a split second, but it was enough to make her smile with small, private triumph. He recovered quickly and barged through the door. She perched on the armchair by the bookcase, where she could see his face when he had to come sheepishly out again. She couldn't wait.

He hadn't ever been in her bedroom before. He would hate the multicolored, handmade quilt and the rainbow of scarves tied around her bedpost. He'd think her framed posters were cheap and her framed earring insane. She was petty enough to be glad she hadn't made her bed today. He'd always been obnoxious about military corners. Her mom had come in and remade Belle's bed nearly every day, just to avoid the row.

Dear God, she even heard him opening the closet. Did he really think her mother would be cowering behind the tennis rackets and trench coats?

Eventually, he had to emerge. In his usual way, he transformed his embarrassment into the only emotion he felt comfortable expressing: anger. It came off him in waves. She could almost smell it.

"Damn it, Belle. I don't have time for this." His breath was heaving, as if he'd been tossing things around. Maybe he'd even bent down and looked under the bed. "She said she was with you this morning. You're going to tell me if that's true, and then you're going to tell me where she is now."

"No, Dad." Belle kept her hands loose and relaxed in her lap, but it took some effort. She hadn't seen her mother in days. "I'm not."

"Because you don't know? Or because you just feel like being a bitch?"

She flinched inwardly. He didn't use words like that. His contempt had always been more subtle, though no less deadly.

It was as if her dad was disintegrating right before her eyes. The shock of discovering the family secrets had taken a toll on all of them, but it had clearly tossed a bomb inside Sam Carson, and he was falling apart from the inside out.

"Because I have too much respect for Mom. She isn't under house arrest. Where she is at any given moment is your business only if she decides to make it so."

Belle thought he might slap her. He clearly thought so, too.

Instead, he turned and left the apartment. He slammed the door so hard the pictures on the wall jumped, and a glass fell over in the sink.

When she heard the last of his footsteps stomping down the stairs, Belle pulled her phone out of her pocket and dialed her mother's number.

But she got no answer, either.

She sat on the edge of the chair, staring at the phone.

What on earth was going on?

CHAPTER NINE

MATT COULDN'T REMEMBER ever working as hard to get anything from a woman as he worked that Monday morning to win a smile from Belle Carson.

He hadn't even needed this much concentrated charm to persuade Tilda Marks to dispose of his virginity for him, back in tenth grade.

Obviously, he'd offended the hell out of Belle at the museum. When she arrived at work, dressed in summer white, with her hair scraped back into a tight twist, she'd looked as rigid and cold as an icicle.

When he called her into his office, to work with him and George on rewriting Nana Lina's speech, she'd appeared at the door with a courteous good-morning about as warm as the canned voice on recorded phone messages. *For fake deference and artificial smiles, please press Zero.*

In his experience, every woman had a defrost button, but he couldn't figure out where hers was. She didn't seem to give a damn when he assured her that the problem with the speech was Nana Lina's proud, prickly personality, not Belle's writing. She ignored his self-effacing jokes. She politely chuckled when he told funny Nana Lina stories, but it wasn't real laughter, just more generic noises.

And then he found it.

She liked to work.

She had a sharp mind, and she loved to use it. Small talk bored her. Empty compliments passed through her. But when they got into the nitty-gritty of reworking the speech, brainstorming new ways to phrase things, new ideas to fit Nana Lina's eccentric style, Belle seemed to completely forget she was angry.

It was fun to watch her. She had this way of sliding her glasses up to her head whenever she was excited about an idea, as if they got in the way of her vision. She did it so often during the meeting that, eventually, tendrils of satiny blond curls escaped the frigid twist, creating a soft halo around her face.

He loved the blinking, slightly myopic look in her blue eyes when she didn't have the glasses on. It made him want to smile, just because it was so misleading. She might look like Red Riding Hood, but she had the brave heart and nimble mind of the wolf.

Her ideas were fantastic. She had a natural ease with words.

They'd been working two hours before the real breakthrough came.

George had suggested a start for a closing remark, thinking out loud, but then floundered. The room was silent a minute. Suddenly, at the precise same moment, Belle and Matt both finished it for him, using exactly the same words.

He laughed. And so did she.

Bingo.

Their eyes met across the desk, and he could tell that she'd forgiven him.

Matt felt George staring at him. He forced himself to look away from Belle, but it was too late. The look on George's face said it all.

He stood abruptly. "Damn it. I'm meeting Ken Castle for lunch. We're going to stop by the film shoot afterward. We've got an appointment with their PR guy. I'd better get going. Think you guys can finish the last page together?"

Matt nodded. Flint Park, where the Hollywood crew was filming, was just at the other end of the block. Finding an entrée into that trend-setting crowd was at the top of Diamante's list.

"Sure. Go for it. Get those pizzas onto that set."

He glanced at Belle, to see whether the idea of working alone with him disconcerted her, but she was already staring down at the speech, chewing on the knuckle of her index finger. That meant, he'd learned, that her mind was working a mile a minute.

He exchanged a grin with George. "We're fine."

When Belle finally looked up, several minutes later, she didn't even seem to notice that George was gone.

"In this part," she said, tapping the last paragraph, "I think my mistake was in shifting the focus away from your grandfather. That's what she's comfortable with, obviously. She doesn't want to blow her own horn, but she wants everyone to know what an amazing man Colm Malone was."

"That's right. And with good reason. My grandfather was one of a kind. He was wise and tough, and yet extraordinarily loving. He and my grandmother married at sixteen, and they had one of those lifelong fairy-tale romances. Except without the sappy part. Nana Lina doesn't believe in sappy."

Belle was watching him, but she'd pushed her glasses up, as if she wanted to be able to see more clearly with her inner eye.

"It sounds beautiful." Her voice was wistful. "I'll bet he never so much as looked at another woman."

"God, no!" Matt laughed. "She would have skinned him alive. But there wasn't much chance of that, anyhow. Other women were invisible to him."

For some reason, that seemed to make Belle sad. He wondered why. But then he remembered that handsome, blustering man who had come to see her. Her arrogant, bullying father. Maybe there wasn't a lot of love and fidelity in the Carson household.

"They were lucky," he said. "Not everyone finds a soul mate at sixteen, or even at sixty. Most of us have to limp on, just doing the best we can, trying not to hurt or get hurt…not too much, anyhow."

She nodded slowly. "I guess that's true." She cleared her throat, as if she'd realized the conversation had turned far too personal. She picked up her pencil. "Okay, so how about if we say something like—"

His cell phone had to pick that moment to ring. Damn it. It wasn't a number he gave out to the public, so it couldn't be ignored. But if it was Colby, Matt was going to kill him.

It wasn't Colby. In fact, he didn't recognize the caller on the display. He tried to think whether there was any way Tiffani could have gotten hold of this number, but decided it was unlikely.

"Sorry," he said to Belle, who put down her pen and started to get up.

"No," he said, waving her back down. "Wait. I won't be a minute. I'd like to get this done today."

As she lowered herself back onto the chair, he picked up.

"Matt Malone," he said, hoping the crisp tone of a busy man at work would discourage any telemarketers.

"Mr. Malone." It was a woman, probably middle-aged. Slight accent, smoker's rasp. He didn't recognize her. Not a telemarketer, though. None of the phony, ingratiating cheer.

"This is Matt Malone," he repeated.

"Okay. Umm…Mr. Malone, you don't know me, but my husband used to work for you. He doesn't anymore, thank God, but I thought you should hear about this. Your guy who gives out the money, that Mr. Kirkman?"

"You mean Mr. Kirkland? Our Drivers Fund manager?"

Matt noticed that Belle's pencil stilled when he said Todd's name. She had been aware of how drunk Todd was the other night, of course.

"Yes. Todd Kirkland," the woman on the other end said. "He's a bad man. He doesn't care about people who are hurting."

Matt's hand tightened on the phone. "And what did you say your name was? Mrs.…?"

"I didn't. I'm not going to give you my name, because I don't want you to come after me. Or my husband. I just thought someone should speak up. About Mr. Kirkland. You heard what I said, right?"

Matt wondered if he could get the number traced. "Yes, I heard you. But I'm not sure why you think so. Do you have some reason to believe such a thing? Do you have any proof of wrongdoing?"

She laughed, an angry sound that ended in a cough. "*Proof?* Where is somebody like me going to get proof? Maybe you don't care about people who're hurting, either. My husband says you're different, but I don't know."

He pulled out a pen. "Okay, Mrs.... Why don't you give me a number where I can reach you, and I—"

But she was already gone.

He looked at the phone, a tight feeling spreading across his chest. He had no idea whether the woman's accusation had any basis. It could easily just be the nastiest kind of character assassination. Since the Drivers Fund had been created, there had been quite a few requests that Todd had to deny, and many of the rejected didn't take it gracefully.

The fund had been set up to help Diamante employees facing true emergencies. Overextending your credit cards for a plasma TV didn't qualify. Neither did huge speeding tickets, or more exotic vacations.

So this woman's vitriol could have been prompted by anything. But Matt didn't like coincidences, and the call followed awfully hard on the heels of Todd's breakdown the other night.

Matt shut the phone off. He drummed his fingers on the arm of his chair for a minute, trying to think.

"Is everything all right?"

He looked across the desk to where Belle was watching him, her eyes intelligent and curious behind her glasses. He should have let her leave before he took the call. She'd obviously heard enough to deduce that someone had accused Todd of something.

Matt had an absurd impulse to tell her exactly what had happened.

It was selfish, but it would be nice to have someone objective to talk it over with. Both he and Nana Lina were too fond of Todd, too sorry for the mess his life had become. Colby and Red were too hostile.

Belle would be neutral. She was smart. She was a decent judge of people. And she wasn't petty. He'd truly like to know what she thought.

But of course he couldn't do that. If Todd had indeed gone off the rails, Matt wasn't going to shame him by making the failure public. If Todd hadn't done anything wrong, if this caller was just motivated by disappointed greed, then the fewer people who heard the accusations the better.

Matt knew what to do, anyhow. It involved hiring an auditor. It would hurt Todd's feelings, but it had to be done.

"Yes," he said after too long a wait. "Everything is fine."

"Maybe I should go?" Belle put her paperwork into a neat pile and made a motion as if to get up.

This time he didn't stop her. "All right," he said. "I'm sure you can finish the rest. Thanks for all your hard work. It's going to be a great speech."

She smiled, not the warm grin he'd been so proud of

eliciting earlier. But not the phone-lady smile, either. He had made a little progress, then.

Belle got up and moved to the door, her white dress swirling slightly around her knees. Her legs were—

Damn it, Malone.... He dragged his gaze back up to her face.

"I'll e-mail you a revised version," she said. "When I'm done."

"Fine." He hesitated. "And, Belle…"

She waited, her hand on the knob.

"I just wanted to say I'm sorry. About what I said the other night. I trust you completely. I know perfectly well you weren't trying to get a job with Drayson."

The apology had sprung to his lips impulsively. He hadn't thought it through, had no idea how she would respond. But whatever he'd been expecting, the uncomfortable look that crossed her face wasn't it.

He couldn't tell exactly what the hastily smothered expression meant. It could have been embarrassment, guilt, disapproval or fear.

The only thing he knew for certain was that it wasn't delight. For some reason, his apology did not make her happy.

For several seconds, she didn't speak.

"It's all right," she said finally. "You don't have to be sorry. It's probably not smart to trust anyone *completely,* is it? One thing I learned in the short time I was a journalist is that deep inside…"

He waited.

She shrugged. "Deep inside, everyone's motives are a little murky."

BY FRIDAY EVENING BELLE was exhausted, and when the phone rang in the Diamante office, she almost didn't answer it.

She'd worked sixty hours this week, planning the launch events. Not that she really minded. She was learning so much—everything from where to get the best novelty giveaways, to which permits were required to sell food on the beach—that sometimes she thought her head might explode.

She hadn't been able to spare even a minute to search for information about Todd Kirkland, and she had to admit she was secretly relieved. The whole subject of Todd made her edgy, even though that weird phone call in Matt's office Monday morning certainly raised more red flags. Still, she couldn't make up her mind what was right.

So she threw herself into the coming launch instead. She fell into bed each night mentally writing the leads of the next day's press releases, and she dreamed of plastic rings nestled inside Cinnamon Diamond desserts.

She also hadn't been able to talk alone with her mother, to find out what had happened last Sunday. She knew her mom was fine, and she'd received half a dozen promises of a call when a moment of privacy presented itself, but so far…nothing.

Maybe Belle should have pushed harder, insisted on a full-out discussion of Adam, her dad's fury and her mother's secrecy. But she needed a drama-free environment while she mastered this job, so she ignored the inner voice that warned about the calm that always came before the storm.

The phone kept ringing, like a pin poked in her conscience. She sighed, swiveled her chair and went over to Francie's desk.

"Diamante Incorporated. This is Isabelle."

There was a pause. Then Matt spoke. "Belle? What are you doing in the office so late?"

"Just finishing up some details. Is there something I can do for you?"

He groaned. "Not unless you know how to wait tables. I was thinking Francie might still be there."

"Wait tables? What's going on?"

"Pure bedlam. I'm in the restaurant, downstairs. We're having what you might call a movie-star emergency."

"Oh! Did they finally agree to let you cater something for them?"

"Not really. Apparently their regular caterer ran into a hitch. They just showed up at the door. Fifty of them. All starving. And not the most patient people in the world." He laughed. "We've called in everyone on the payroll, but there's no way—"

"I can come down."

He paused. "No, really, Belle, you don't have to—"

"I want to. We've been trying all week to get in with the movie crew. This is our chance." She chuckled. "What? Are you afraid I'll spill coffee all over the director?"

"The director's so drunk he'd never notice. If you're willing, that would be wonderful. Come on down!"

Bedlam was an understatement.

She could barely squeeze through the front door, so many people were jammed up against it. In the center of the long, brick-floored room, the cast and their crew held court. Someone had a guitar. The lead actress, not an A-list star, but definitely a B-plus, stood on a table, singing "O Sole Mio." She was okay, actually, but her costar, who had decided to dance along with the music, definitely shouldn't give up acting.

Around them, regular customers ogled and craned their necks so that they wouldn't miss a second. Belle wondered how on earth she'd ever find Matt in the chaos.

"You must be Belle!" A gorgeous young man grabbed her by the shoulders and kissed her cheek with enthusiasm. "Bless you, you beautiful creature! I'm Red, and we're absolutely desperate! Go straight to the kitchen. Grab an apron and a pad, and as many water glasses as you can carry. Start passing them out to anyone who doesn't have one."

She nodded, dazed by the energy the man gave off. As quickly as she could, she sidestepped and wriggled her way through the crowd toward what she hoped was the kitchen. Two swinging doors, one hard shove and finally she was in.

Not that it was any less hectic in here. Four men in white were working like a synchronized dance team, wielding long-handled implements, sliding pizzas into and pulling them out of the wood-burning ovens faster than seemed possible.

Off to the side, three other men were kneading, pounding and shaping dough. One of them was Matt.

He looked up and grinned. "Reinforcements!" He elbowed the man standing next to him. "Colby, this is Belle."

Colby smiled. Then Matt turned his head, though his

hands kept deftly moving through the dough. "Nana Lina! Belle is here!"

Oh, God. Her stomach swooped. She had expected to work among a bunch of the restaurant's other employees, in comfortable anonymity. She had no idea the whole family was here.

The beautiful older woman she'd seen at the party came gliding around a corner, apparently the only one immune to the chaos. Her hair framed her face in perfect white waves, and over her black dress she wore a crisp white apron with delicate green embroidery along the edges.

"No," she said firmly as she passed Colby. She halted his hand on the measuring cup. "Since you were six, always too much flour."

Then, as Colby laughed and set the cup down, she extended a slim hand to Belle. "It is very generous of you to come, Belle. It's not easy work, and these customers have no manners. But they will have the best pizza in San Francisco, if I can persuade my grandson to stop adding flour with a shovel."

Looking into those amused chocolate-brown eyes, Belle realized that she'd do a lot more than fill water glasses if this woman asked her to. No wonder Colm Malone hadn't been able to see any other women.

Belle tried not to compare that relationship to her own grandparents'. Women other than his wife hadn't been invisible to Grandpa Robert, had they? He'd slept with another woman, maybe for years, while he was married to Sarah. He'd even fathered children by that woman. So what had gone wrong? Was the fault in Robert? Or in Sarah?

Or was it unfair to try to affix blame, so many years later, with so much left unexplained?

"I'm delighted to meet you, Mrs. Malone. I'm not sure how much help I'll be, but I'm happy to try."

"My grandson tells me you're a very fast learner. My husband used to say a willing heart and a sensible mind can do anything." She picked up a tray and handed it to Belle with a wink. "However, in this case a pair of strong arms and a high tolerance for fools would be even more useful."

The next three hours flew by. As word got out that the film people were here, Diamante's large dining area filled to overflowing. Soon a line formed at the door, but no one who was already inside had any intention of leaving. They had to order something to justify hanging around star watching, so Belle quickly graduated from water girl to waitress.

Even during her waitressing days in college, she'd never worked so hard in her life. By the end of the first hour, her shoulders ached and her feet throbbed inside her sensible pumps. Thank heaven she hadn't decided to wear a pair of Pandora's "fun" shoes today!

By the end of the second hour, every inch of her body had gone numb.

But she was having the time of her life. At her house, this level of stress would have sent her dad into a rage long ago. Her mother would either have retired to weep alone, or worked on in stoic silence, sacrificing herself on the altar of family peace.

Not this family. As the stress increased, they just ramped up the energy and adrenaline. They laughed, they sang songs, they danced around one another in the kitchen and in the dining room. They clearly enjoyed working, and they welcomed a challenge.

And no one got mad when a mistake was made. They rallied around the one who had goofed, joking and sharing their own dumb moments, until any embarrassment was laughed away. When Belle compared that to the disgusted criticism that followed any errors at the Carson household...

It seemed as if she had stumbled into an alternate universe. A fairy-tale world, where the very air was flavored with joy, and hard work became a game. Where everyone was on the same team, and no matter what happened, you won.

Every time she delivered an order to the kitchen, she found her gaze drawn to Matt and Colby, who seemed so at home, standing at the counter kneading dough, rolling it out, even now and then tossing it in the air while the others whistled and laughed. They applied pepperoni slices like Las Vegas croupiers dealing cards, and sprinkled onions, mushrooms and crumbled beef through expert fingers.

Of course, they were at home. They'd grown up helping out here, and probably tossing pizzas at home, as well. This was the family tradition.

Through all the take-out expansions, this charming brick-and-wood space, made out of the first floor of a whole block of town houses, remained the one and only sitdown Diamante restaurant. The walls were covered with pictures of celebrities who sent their love to Lina, as well as family pictures that took Colm and Angelina, their son, and finally the three grandsons through all the stages of life.

At the end of three hours, Belle almost felt like one of the family. She had picked up their serenity, and didn't even get rattled when a fussy customer demanded a special pizza. Mushrooms applied first, cooked briefly, then followed five minutes later by onions, but only yellow onions, and they must be slivered, not chopped, about as thick as your pinky finger.

Wow. The kitchen had openings at each end, and she entered by the one nearest Matt and Colby. She read off the woman's insane list of requirements to Matt, who was standing nearest to the door. He listened, though his hands never paused, deftly spreading marinara sauce over the dough he'd just shaped into a pan.

She apologized for the intricacy of the order, but he just smiled. "That's Mrs. Tarkington," he said. "We've been making that pizza for years."

He glanced toward the other counter, where his grandmother was supervising the mixing of more dough for tomorrow, as they'd undoubtedly use everything they had tonight. "Nana Lina, where do you keep the Tarkington onions these days?"

His grandmother didn't even turn around. "Top left. But she was here yesterday, so we may be out."

"Dang it," Colby grumbled. "Wouldn't you know it?"

"Grab a knife and cut some, you lazy boys." Angelina's dry voice was amused. "Unless now that you're so expensively educated, you've forgotten how to perform even the simplest practical task."

The brothers exchanged looks, and Colby reached for

a couple of yellow onions and a knife. "God, she's a tyrant, isn't she?"

Matt winked at Belle, brushing flour from his cheek with his free hand. "Promise me something, Belle. When we get back to the office on Monday, swear that you'll erase the memory of my grandmother bossing me around like a naughty little boy."

"Sorry," Belle said, shaking her head and trying not to grin. She slipped Mrs. Tarkington's order into the overhead slot. "I have a photographic memory. This image is burned in my brain for all time."

"Oh, yeah?" Matt tilted his head. "Actually, that doesn't sound all bad, now that I think about it."

Colby made a small snorting sound, which he covered up quickly. "Excuse me," he said with exaggerated innocence. "Something in my throat."

"I am not," Angelina said crisply, "paying the three of you to stand around flirting."

Matt laughed out loud as he slipped a pizza peel under the pie he'd just created and handed it off to the bakers. "You're not paying us at all, you slave driver."

"That is entirely beside the point."

She wiped her hands on her apron, then stepped closer and took hold of Belle's hands gently.

"I've been watching you, my dear. I like you. You have character. So I'll be honest. My grandsons already operate under the delusion that they are irresistible. I'm counting on you to give them…shall we call it a reality check? Ignore them. It will do them a world of good."

"Yes, ma'am," Belle said, feeling her cheeks flush with irrational pleasure. Warmth trickled through her

like the honey that was the secret ingredient of Diamante's pizza crust.

She turned to Matt with a grin. "Have to get back to
work. Sorry, boss. I report to a higher power now."

CHAPTER TEN

HE HAD DRAWN THE LINE at wearing swim trunks.

He was as determined as anyone to make a success of this event, the first of the beach parties designed to launch a new franchise. He'd said yes to almost everything Belle and George suggested. He had agreed to give away Cinnamon Diamonds, and he had agreed to donate one hundred percent of his pizza profits. He had approved radio interviews, and he didn't complain about the radio van broadcasting pop music right there beside them on the sand. With his permission, they'd sent free pizzas to the stations all week, drumming up excitement.

And he was devoting his whole day to the darn thing. He had accepted the need to personally hand out pizzas in the hot sun.

But he was *not* willing to become the feature act in a beefcake show.

Francie had taken up a petition at work, just to devil him, and everyone, even the computer techies, had signed it twice. When they heard about the controversy, Colby and Red had presented him with a thong swimsuit that had a very unusual crotch, which promised to lift and enhance. The bastards had almost broken ribs laughing at the look on Matt's face when he opened it.

Well, they could enjoy the joke while it lasted. When Matt arrived at the little half-moon bay where the event would take place, he wore blue jeans, a yellow T-shirt and a navy jacket. He was the boss. They could just live with it.

Belle greeted him in the parking lot, clipboard in hand. She looked absolutely fantastic in a sleeveless yellow sundress, short enough to tickle the tops of her knees, and sandals that made her pink-tipped toes look X-rated. Her hair was loosely tied back with a white ribbon, but was already spinning free around the edges and dancing in the breeze.

She looked professional, but still…the minute you saw her you started thinking of hot sex in the sand.

He'd been worrying for nothing. He could have come out here stark naked and no one would have noticed him. Not with Belle around.

"We've got quite a crowd already," she said, running her pencil down the list on the clipboard as they walked toward the beach. "You have your first interview, with WWHM, in about five minutes. Then one with the guy from the local paper…he's the one over there in all black. Then you're on pizza duty for about two hours, with five-minute breaks every thirty minutes for other interviews."

She grinned like a kid who brought home all A's. "That's pretty good, isn't it? Sundays are fantastic for this kind of thing. Slow news days. The TV stations, especially, will bite at any piece of fluff you offer on a Sunday."

He smiled. "Hey, now. Don't flatter me like that. I might start thinking I'm important."

"Oh, I—" She groaned, but then started laughing. "Well, I'm sorry, but it's true. Don't pretend you didn't already know that a guy handing out free cinnamon rolls on the beach isn't exactly the Pulitzer Prize exposé of the year."

"No," Matt said with a one-sided smile. "I had no idea. I'm crushed."

She groaned and flipped her legal pad shut. He loved it that she no longer cowered. Partly, the difference was that she was growing into the job, soaking up information from George like a sponge and gaining confidence every day.

But the night they'd slaved together serving pizza to bratty movie stars had somehow been a turning point. Now she was more comfortable around him.

It was almost like being friends.

He put his hand under her arm, pretending he thought she might need help with her balance as they picked their way across the soft sand between the dunes. He had always thought guys who did that were losers, but now he saw how useful chivalry could be.

They reached the Diamante table and trailer far too soon. He would have liked to walk right on past it, his hand still tucked into that warm, satiny place inside her elbow. And then he'd like to keep walking until they ran out of beach.

Instead, he had to let go. About two dozen beachgoers with pink shoulders and wet, sandy hair, stood around waiting to see what was going to happen. Most of the males, young and old, seemed to be watching Belle. Even a punk little kid of maybe twelve was staring at her with his mouth open, as if she were better than a big, sweet lollipop. Ordinarily, Matt liked kids, but that one got on his nerves.

Belle didn't seem self-conscious about her audience. She smiled at everyone, even as she made her way quickly up to the guy with a microphone who stood beside the big, tacky WWHM van.

She chatted with him as if he were her best friend, when really he was an overweight noise box with a balding head and a face definitely made for radio. The boss in Matt appreciated how quickly she was mastering the skill of artful networking. But the male in him thought she should back down the charm. The WWHM guy was too old and too fat to get this kind of jolt to the libido.

She led the disc jockey over to him. "Mr. Malone, this is Andy in the Afternoon, from WWHM. He's broadcasting from the event today, and he'd like to start by talking to you for a few minutes."

She gave the man a smile, full of understanding camaraderie. "He knows you've got another interview in ten minutes, and some hungry people here, too, who are all hoping the pizza sales will start on time."

She moved away diplomatically, and made her way to the Goth-looking kid who passed for a local reporter around here. The kid was talking to Belle's cleavage, the little—

Just in time, Matt recognized how negative his attitude was, and why. He pulled himself up hard. Doing the jealous-male routine in front of a dozen cameras would be dumb beyond belief.

He turned on the switch that had seen him through a million meetings, parties and interviews in the past. He held out his hand and shook the other man's beefy paw.

"Hey, Andy. Thanks so much for coming by. It's going to add a lot to the event, having your station here."

Matt kept his focus all day. He handled Andy in the Afternoon, Proud Mary from WMIX, and a parade of other small-paper and TV reporters who pretty much all asked the same questions. By the end of the day, he was straining to think of another way to say "excited about the expansion" or "so proud to donate to this excellent charity."

The turnout was respectable. He sold about three hundred pizzas to college students and families with hungry kids, two groups guaranteed to be attracted by freebies. Even better, they all seemed to love the food, which boded well for the franchise's future.

Beside him, one of the pretty young managers from the new franchise handed out the free Cinnamon Diamonds, along with an explanation of the special diamond ring promotion. Of the three hundred cinnamon rolls, ten percent had rings planted inside, a number George had decided on as plentiful enough to sustain hope, but rare enough to create excitement.

Now and then a squeal and a cheer would go up, indicating another prize discovered. Business always picked up a little right after that, the curious drawn in by the noise.

The marketing company handling the larger sweepstakes had sent a rep to help with the entries. Together the rep and a couple of waitresses from the downtown Diamante took information from all the winners, to make sure they got their bonus entries submitted.

Belle was never near enough to talk to, except when she brought the next reporter up to interview Matt, or ushered the last one away so that he could go back to selling. She had a million details to oversee, and she never stayed in one place for long. But somehow, through it all, he managed to keep her in his peripheral vision, as if she were a flickering yellow sunbeam dancing on the horizon.

They sold the last pizza just as the sun was dropping low enough to sizzle slightly on the water. He gave his last interview with the colorful sunset as a background, and then he went to find Belle.

She was in the vending trailer, thanking the two chefs who had kept the hot pizzas coming. They'd all been premade back at the new franchise, of course, but someone had to keep them hot, out of the sun and ready to distribute.

"Belle? Got a minute?"

She turned around. "Sure." She looked slightly edgy. "Did that last interview go all right? I didn't come out to remind him time was up because he said it was going to be live, and usually that means they—"

"It went fine. No problems with any of that. I wanted to talk to you about something else."

"Oh. Okay."

She stepped carefully out of the trailer, saying her goodbyes to the men inside. The air had grown nippy since the sun began to sink. She shivered as a breeze cut past them.

"I knew I should have worn something else." She grinned, chafing her upper arms. "My friend Pandora gives the world's worst advice about clothes."

Matt wanted to tell her that wasn't true, that Pandora was a genius, but some remnant of common sense stopped him. He took off his jacket and draped it around Belle's shoulders, which maybe wasn't too smart, either. It clearly surprised her, and the sight of it swamping her small frame was shockingly intimate.

"You can't concentrate if you're freezing to death," he said, in a lame attempt to make it sound like a business-related loan. "It might take a few minutes, what I wanted to talk to you about."

"Okay," she said slowly. "What is it?"

"I've heard from Nana Lina. I sent her a copy of the speech you wrote." He turned his back on the trailer and started to walk, feeling the urge to get away from the table where he'd been dispensing pizzas for so long. Belle automatically kept pace with him. "I thought we should go over what she said."

Belle looked up at him, her hair on fire in the peach-colored sunset. "Oh, dear. Did she hate it?"

"No, no. For the most part, she was quite happy with it. She had a couple of problems with the middle. You remember—that part was from the first version. We suspected it might still be a little too personal. I thought it was worth a shot, but she's already put a big red X through it."

Belle laughed. "I knew she wouldn't go for it. Once I met her, I realized that the speech I originally wrote was all wrong."

"Well, you fixed that. Amazingly, with that one ex-

ception, she's approved the whole thing. That's damn
rare, with Nana Lina. Ask George. He's had to rewrite
some press releases five, six, even seven times before
she's happy."

Belle did a little skip on the sand to demonstrate her
delight. Matt caught the scent of her perfume, drifting
alongside the salty brine of the ocean. To his horror, he
felt his groin tighten.

He should get out of here. He should take his jacket
and go home.

Before he did something really stupid.

"Belle." He stopped. They hadn't gone more than
about five hundred feet, but the people back at the site
were silhouetted against the sunset, oddly anonymous
and faraway. He turned toward her. He could barely
make out her features in the dying light, but even so,
arousal shot through him like a lust-tipped arrow.

"Belle…"

"Yes?" She sounded slightly breathless. He wondered whether she could feel it, too. Something arcing
between them, tugging at thoughts they both knew they
shouldn't be having.

The wind had kicked up harder, and his coat made a
ruffling sound, ballooning out around her. Her yellow
skirt lifted, as if unseen hands had slipped under it.

He couldn't control what was happening to him. His
jeans tightened, and his heart was like a drumbeat, insisting, insisting.

Her hair feathered against her cheeks, her lips, her
eyes. He reached out and brushed it away, just to feel
the silk of her face under his fingertips.

"I've been meaning to thank you," he said, his voice husky. "For everything you've done since you joined us. I know it wasn't a job you particularly wanted, but you've really put your heart into it."

"I love it," she said. Her voice was breathy, too, and she didn't pull away from his fingers, even though he'd left them there, just under her ear. It was as if they were having one conversation and their bodies were having another.

"Do you?"

She nodded against his hand. "Yes. I'm beginning to, I mean. So much…so much more than I thought I would."

"I'm glad." He would have said more, but didn't want to talk. He wanted…

He lowered his face toward hers. He went slowly, agonizingly slowly, so that she would have time to stop him. He felt the warmth of her body rising to meet him, and he sensed when she tipped her face toward him, just a fraction of an inch, but enough to send the signal.

Yes. Yes.

After that, nothing could have stopped him. He held her chin with both hands, as if her heart-shaped face were a cup from which he needed desperately to drink. He touched her mouth softly at first, and then let the kiss deepen, until he heard her make a low sound, and felt her lips part beneath his.

He drove in, then, with all the painful need that had been shooting through him…perhaps since the first moment he saw her. It made very little sense. But she did things to him, dark, inexplicable things that had nothing to do with logic.

He knew her lips. He'd kissed them in his dreams. It

was almost too much to bear, having it finally be real. But it was. He tasted the cinnamon that had dusted the corners of her smile, and the darker, muskier sweetness that was hers alone. It was a familiar taste, as if he'd known her forever, as if her mouth had belonged to him always.

It was how longing had always felt, and smelled, and tasted, in his soul.

She put the heels of her hands on his chest.

It was the universal sign of a woman who wanted to stop. He let go of her immediately, though his pulse was still throbbing heavily in his throat.

"Belle?"

"I'm sorry…it's just that—" She seemed to be having trouble finding words. She kept taking breaths and starting over. Her round eyes looked slightly dazed. "I don't think we should—"

"Of course. You're right. I'm sorry."

Damn it. What had he done? He inhaled air as far down into his lungs as he could, trying to clear his head. He backed up a step, hoping it might help if he wasn't still close enough to smell her perfume mingling with the scent of him, carried on his coat.

"That was incredibly dumb," he said. "I guess I just got carried away. The day…how well everything went…"

The way she looked in that dress, the music of her voice, the competent way she held her clipboard against her high, firm breasts…

"I know. I know. Me, too." She laughed awkwardly, trying to cooperate in this hollow explanation they both knew was fictitious. She held her hands up, trying to contain her flyaway hair, as if that represented everything that had spiraled out of control here. "I think I was a little drunk on my first success."

"You have every right to be." His tones sounded more normal now, he noticed with grim relief. The note of formality was just right. "You did a fantastic job."

"Thanks." She glanced back at the trailer. Only a few people still remained, dark shadows bustling about. "Well. I guess I should get back and help them break everything down."

"Yes. And I have a meeting." It was true. He had completely forgotten. He'd been supposed to dart away from this event as soon as the last pizza was sold. "I really am grateful for all your hard work, Belle, even if I did pick…an inappropriate way to show it."

"It's all right," she said brightly. "I understand."

"You don't have to worry. It won't happen again."

She smiled. "Of course not. I know." She slipped his jacket off her shoulders and handed it back to him. "Thanks. It helped a lot."

He nodded. Then he stood at the water's edge, watching her as she walked away. The balloon of the sun had deflated, and was bobbing helplessly on the edge of the horizon. When her shadow blended with the others, and he could no longer be sure which one was hers, he turned the other direction and circled back to his car the long way.

When he got in and shut the door, he bent his head once to the jacket and inhaled the last lingering hint of her. Then he wadded up the fabric roughly, tossed it into the back and entered Cindi Sullivan's address into his GPS. Forget the meeting. He would never be able to concentrate anyhow.

He'd damn near lost his mind tonight.

He couldn't let it happen again.

And, as Colby always said, the shortest route to sanity usually went straight through another beautiful woman.

CHAPTER ELEVEN

A QUIET DRINK WITH Sue was exactly what Belle needed.

They settled for meeting after Belle got off work, at the little bar across the street from the Diamante complex. Neither of them had much time for a leisurely dinner these days. Sue had always been busy with the babies she fostered, but now that she was married, and they had adopted Rick's niece, Carrie, girl-time was more elusive than ever.

"Oh, my gosh, Belle," Sue said as they took their white wine to a small iron table on the sidewalk. "Is that an engagement ring?"

Belle grinned, holding out her hand. She'd worn one of the Cinnamon Diamond prize rings, just for the fun of seeing Sue's face in that split second before she realized it was a toy.

"Nope. It's the ring we're hiding in the dessert pastries. Part of Diamante's Diamond Sweepstakes. But it looks pretty impressive for plastic, doesn't it? We really worked to strike the perfect balance between price and pizzazz."

Sue studied the ring. "Very sparkly. And as long as the lighting is very, very dim…" She let go. "Darn. I thought maybe you'd landed that hunky, eligible boss of yours."

Belle took a sip of wine. "Nope. Besides, Matt Malone is the ultimate alpha male. I don't do alpha males, remember?"

"Maybe not. I blame your dad for that particular little neurosis. But the cutest *beta* guy on the planet asked you to marry him, and you didn't want him, either."

Belle sighed and leaned back against the cool metal of the chair. She considered explaining about Matt Malone, and the amazing, confusing kiss they'd shared on the beach four days ago. But she wasn't sure she was ready to talk about that with anyone. She had a hard time even thinking about it, without feeling weak and utterly bewildered.

It was already Wednesday, and Matt hadn't shown up at work this week. She had to admit she was relieved. Could she have looked him calmly in the eye and talked about cheese vendors, city permits and media lists?

But why hadn't he come? Was he regretting the kiss that profoundly? Was he avoiding her, for fear she'd read too much into it, and expect to be promoted to vice president?

Sue straightened her ponytail, still smiling. "So now what, romantically? Total chastity? The Sisters of Mercy?"

"How about *nobody?* Temporary chastity? How about I concentrate on this new career of mine and see if I can make a go of it?"

"Makes sense to me. I'm the last one to push anyone into romance. You know how long I insisted I'd never get married." Sue glanced down at her left hand, as if it still surprised and thrilled her just to see the ring there.

Then she pulled herself back into the moment. "Okay. I can't stay long. Carrie is catching something, and Rick's a nervous wreck. So don't waste a minute. Tell me what else is going on."

Belle looked at the amber lights glowing from the windows of Diamante's, directly across the street. Sue had suggested meeting there—Diamante's wine list was famous—but Belle had resisted. An ultrasensible woman, Sue never pushed. If you explained, fine. If you didn't, she let it go.

"Well," Belle said, "after all this time of having my invitations ignored, I got a very strange visit from Joe Fraser the other day."

"Really?" Sue frowned. "Strange how?"

"He wants me to stop my mother from visiting his dad in the hospital. He said she was upsetting him."

Sue, who knew as well as anyone how gentle and benign Emily Carson was, looked appropriately startled. "Okay…let's start with the most obvious shocker. Your mom is visiting Adam? Is your dad aware of it?"

"Nope. She asked me not to tell him. I feel strange about it, since he's issued a royal decree that we're not to associate with any of the Frasers. Mostly I'm just trying to stay out of it."

"Excellent plan. But what's this nonsense about Emily upsetting Adam? She hasn't upset anyone in her life. Luckily, I think Adam gets out pretty soon—he may be out already. I don't know how Joe will cope with that. He and his dad have some serious issues. That's probably why he's so uptight about visitors."

Belle nodded. "I thought maybe it was something like that. My mom could never really cause trouble."

"Now if it were your *dad*… That would be another

story." Sue shook her head. She had been in Belle's stress-laden house often enough, from childhood on. No secrets among cousins.

"He's positively crazed about the heart diamond, as I'm sure you know." Sue swirled her wine. "Guess what he said to Mom, when she called to tell him she was heading back to Florida?"

Belle cringed. "I have no idea. Something hideous, I assume?"

"Yeah. He reminded her that Sarah's revelations meant nothing. He is still the only *legitimate* Carson heir. He said his father had intended him to have that diamond, and that if Mom accepted it under these terms, she was not only a bastard, she was a common thief."

Belle put her palm over her wineglass and lowered her head to her hand. "Oh, my God. I'm so sorry, Sue. I don't know what's gotten *into* him."

"Greed? Spite?" Sue shrugged. "Sorry. That wasn't very nice."

"That's okay. I understand how you must feel. Your mother isn't going to let him have it, is she?"

"No way. She gave it to me because she has a soft spot for Sam, in spite of everything. I, on the other hand, am pure granite where this is concerned. Mom doesn't care much about the diamond itself—she's not particularly materialistic. But I've convinced her that she can't let Sam bully her. Sarah…Sarah wanted *her* to have it."

Sue's normally cool demeanor cracked a bit as she spoke her grandmother's name. Belle had adored Grandma Sarah, too, but for some reason Sarah and Sue had always had a special bond. Belle could only imagine what it had felt like for Sue to learn that her mother, Jenny, had been the love child of Robert Carson's mistress.

Though Sarah had obviously loved Jenny, her emotions must have been complicated. Had there been moments, after she adopted the child born of betrayal, when she was filled with anger and pain? Had Jenny, and then Jenny's daughter, Sue, been daily reminders of Robert Carson's broken vows and his eternally divided heart?

These questions would undoubtedly haunt Sue now, too.

"Sue," Belle began.

"I'm fine." But Sue's eyes glistened under the streetlights, and she looked away for a second, swallowing hard. "It's just that…this was Sarah's last wish, and I'll throw the darn thing into the Pacific before I'll let Sam take it away."

"I'll help," Belle said. She put her hand over her cousin's. "Or maybe we should just bury it by the Golden Gate Bridge, so that someday we can dig it up and—"

But then, across the street, she saw something that created a roadblock of emotions, crashing into one another like bumper cars. No words could possibly get through.

Across the street, walking toward Diamante's warm, honeyed windows…

Matt and Colby Malone.

And beside them, hanging on their strong arms and giggling at their adorable Malone Brothers comedy routine, glided two of the most gorgeous women Belle had ever seen. Two glittering Scandinavian princesses, nearly as tall as the men and shaped like life-size Barbies.

Matt opened the door, standing deferentially to the side while the ladies floated through. Belle would bet a week's salary that those two wouldn't be filling water glasses and waiting tables.

It was ridiculous, the way her heart seemed to be beating from the soles of her shoes.

"What's wrong?" Sue looked over her shoulder, but there was nothing left to see. The charmed quartet had already entered the magic portal and been swallowed up by the festive crowd inside.

"Nothing," Belle said, dragging her gaze away. "Just a random thought about alpha men. Now…you've got a sick baby to get home to, so let's get serious." She grinned evilly at her cousin. "How are we going to make sure my dad doesn't get hold of that diamond?"

BY TWELVE-THIRTY THAT night, Matt's arms ached from shoulder to fingertip, and he suddenly realized he'd been buffing the same spot on the *MacGregor's* hull for…God only knew how long.

He yanked down the battery-operated retractable reel light and aimed it at the boat's side, just to be sure he hadn't buffed right through the fiberglass. It looked fine.

Rocking onto his heels, he used the back of his hand to wipe the sweat from his forehead. Hard work was the best therapy, and the boathouse at midnight was a nice, quiet place to toil off some tension.

But maybe he needed to give it a rest.

Plus, someone was coming. He'd been unaware of

anything for at least an hour now, but in this momentary lull, he could clearly hear footsteps on the dock.

He knew it was Colby even before his brother's dark head appeared in the doorway. Red, an obsessive Giants fan, was at a postgame party, and Nana Lina was out dancing with her new suitor, Sean, a younger man of about seventy-five.

The footsteps were too heavy to belong to a female, and too relaxed for an axe-murderer.

Therefore…Colby.

"Wow." Colby's gaze took in the cloudy fiberglass, the tub of wax, the dirty chamois and Matt's sweaty work clothes. "When the instructions say 'do not wax your boat in broad daylight,' you take that pretty seriously, don't you? Don't you realize it's after midnight?"

"Hey, Col." Matt smiled at his brother, then picked up his chamois and began buffing again. It gave him somewhere else to direct his eyes. "It's only Wednesday, right? I thought you were staying in town this week."

All three of the Malone grandsons had their own places near downtown, near the restaurant, which they used during the workweek. But most weekends found them here, in Marin County, just over the bridge, at the rambling waterfront house they'd lived in ever since their parents' death.

Colby came in, bumping the bare overhead bulb. Strange shadows pitched and swayed across the walls, like the ghosts of drunken sailors.

"Yeah, well, I was going to. But that was before my hot date went rather abruptly cold."

Matt kept buffing, though until the lightbulb settled

down he could hardly see a thing. "Why? At dinner, I got the impression Stephanie was enjoying herself...and you. What doused the fire?"

"Let's see." Colby pretended to think. "Oh, yeah. That would be you."

"Me?" Finally, Matt met his brother's eyes. "How? I've been in here for hours."

"Yeah, I know. That's the point. Things had just begun to get interesting for Steph and me, when her cell phone starts going off like the bell at a firehouse. Turns out her friend Cindi got dumped at the doorstep by the guy she'd invited in for coffee." Colby raised one eyebrow. "Can you imagine such a heartless beast?"

"I still don't see why that ruins *your* date."

"Let me explain. One, it's a proven medical fact that a woman scorned will explode unless she can indulge in some serious male-bashing with her best friend. And two, guilt by association. If you're a jerk, then I'm a jerk."

Matt knew all that, of course. He'd felt bad when he left an obviously disappointed and offended Cindi at her door. Not bad for her. Though she was major eye candy, she was also the most artificial, calculating female he'd met in a long time. Compared to Cindi, Tiffani was Mother Teresa.

But he'd known that Colby might be taken down, too. Collateral damage in the war between the sexes.

"I'm sorry," Matt said. "But you know, Col...it might be a blessing in disguise. How long do you want to hang out with a woman like Stephanie, anyhow?"

"I don't know. As long as the sex is off the charts, I guess."

Matt tossed the chamois into the bucket. He was

tired. He'd do the other side tomorrow. "Yeah, well, that's not enough for me anymore."

Colby suddenly dropped the pretence of cynicism. He came over and perched on the edge of the foredeck. The boat rocked gently, black tongues of cold water licking at the white hull.

"So what's really wrong? Is it Belle?"

Matt shrugged. He didn't particularly want to talk about it. What was there to say? He'd promised her it wouldn't happen again, and it wouldn't.

Except, ever since he'd kissed her, he thought about her all the time. Sometimes he even dreamed about her, and in his dreams she got mixed up with the woman from the Halloween party all those years ago. They both projected some kind of intangible quality that spoke of substance. An inner goodness…

For the first time in his life, he craved that.

He screwed the cap tightly on the tub of wax, then tossed it, too, into the bucket. "I don't know. Belle is probably part of it. But it's weird. Sometimes I find myself thinking about…"

He chuckled wryly, listening to how insane he sounded. He'd been about to say that sometimes he found himself thinking about Cleopatra.

"You know. About the night of the Halloween party. I can't figure out why I can't quite let that go. It's been eight years, for God's sake. But what if…"

He looked up into his brother's worried face. "What if, as crazy as it sounds, she was actually the one? There was something about her…She was smart, Col, and feisty. And yet there was this crazy sweetness. She understood everything I was feeling, even though I was too plastered to explain it right."

Colby didn't respond. But he was listening, and his mouth had lost that sardonic twist.

Matt scraped irritably at his fingers, trying to get the wax off. "What if that night, that woman, was my one chance at real happiness? What if everyone else is always going to be...second-string?"

He had expected Colby to scoff. But instead his brother just nodded, with a gravity he rarely displayed. Matt wondered whether he'd hit a nerve. Sometimes, in the haunted hours before the dawn, did Colby think about the black-haired Haley Watson and ask himself the same questions?

"Look. Matt. You've got to deal with this, one way or another. Do you think there's any hope of finding her now?" Colby didn't sound as if he was joking.

"After all these years?"

"I know it's a long shot. You asked everyone we knew at the party back then. You drove us all nuts. But in the end she was pretty much a mystery, right? Maybe you gave up too easily. Now, you could be more serious. I mean...like hire a detective or something."

"Yeah, but even if I did find her...then what?" Matt began to smile, thinking how well that would go over. She'd be screaming "stalker" before he could get the first sentence out.

"Just see where it goes. If you could talk to her now, in broad daylight, in street clothes and stone sober, maybe you'd finally see that it wasn't anything but a Halloween fantasy."

"And then I could move on, you mean."

"Exactly." Colby grinned, obviously tired of solemnity. "And then you could move on. And I could have a normal love life again. Or…wait!"

He stood with a jerk, agitating the sleepy water once again.

"Let's go upstairs right now and dig that damn earring out of your box. That's your problem, I guarantee you. It's like one of those black-magic things that cast a spell on you as long as you own them."

In spite of himself, Matt began to smile, too. "Colby, you're insane."

"No, no. This'll work! We'll take the boat out and toss the earring into the bay. We can have a full-blown ceremony, like when your goldfish died. We'll wait till Red comes home, and he can play something sad on the guitar. I'll recite that 'better to have loved and lost' bit from that sappy poem, and you'll cry like a baby as the earring sinks into the deep. And we'll take pictures of you, so that we can blackmail you later, and…"

But Matt was already out of the boathouse, chuckling, his depression fading away. He was tired now, but in a normal way. He just wanted a peaceful night's sleep with no dreams.

Which, he realized later, was probably all Colby wanted to accomplish in the first place.

CHAPTER TWELVE

BELLE STOOD AT THE back of the hotel meeting room, trying not to beam with pride while Angelina Malone delivered the press-conference speech. The woman was a natural. She must have memorized every word because, although Belle had provided a full script, Angelina never once looked down at her podium.

She should have been an actress. She had the power to make even the least inspired of Belle's sentences sound spontaneous and poetic at the same time. Almost a dozen journalists, some print, some TV, had decided to cover this press conference, and every one of them looked half in love with the old lady.

Matt was here, too.

It was the first time Belle had seen him since the beach event. Halfway through the speech, he caught her eye, smiled and gave her a thumbs-up.

And though she tried to quell it, her heart broke out in sunshine.

After that, she couldn't think of anything else. She watched him as he watched his grandmother, and the adoring pride on his face made her heart beat in tight, glitchy thumps.

Fifteen minutes ago, she'd been determined to forget about a guy who was quite comfortable kissing her senseless one day, then ignoring her for a week, wining and dining a Scandinavian princess instead.

Now…Belle was mush all over again, just from witnessing how much he loved his grandmother.

How could he do this to her? Who was this man?

He refused to fit into any of the pigeonholes she'd used for so long.

On one hand, he was a born alpha. Great looking, and well aware of it. Smart, and unwilling to suffer fools gladly. Arrogant, confident, accustomed to power and control.

On the other, he was as sensitive as any beta she'd ever known. He was humble, always ready to laugh at himself. At home selling pizza to sandy children, or kneading dough in a hot kitchen, with an apron around his waist and flour on his cheek.

But…what about his attitude toward women? That wasn't any easier to classify. Did he objectify them? Exploit them? Maybe. He definitely trended toward centerfolds whose IQs wouldn't get in the way. Was he a wolf, a heartbreaker, the bad boy your mother warned you about? Definitely. Broken hearts probably trailed out like a red carpet behind him.

But he loved his grandmother.

And now his presence, twenty feet across the room, had the power to make Belle's nerves hum with awareness. She squeezed her copy of the speech until the edges grew warm and bent.

How perverse the human heart could be.

Why couldn't she have loved David, who had clearly

adored her? All the things she'd wanted so desperately to feel for him, she'd been unable to summon up. The skittering heart, the flutter in the stomach, the way she could look at something, but see only his face instead…

The shuddering night dreams, the misty daydreams, the physical heat, the delight in his presence, the shadow that fell over her day when he was gone.

She felt those things now.

But, God help her, she felt them for Matt.

She was very much afraid she was falling in love with him. It didn't matter that she didn't fully understand him, couldn't categorize him. It didn't even matter that he clearly wasn't in love with her.

Angelina was winding up. She'd reached the part about her late husband, Colm, and the dream he had cooked up in the kitchenette of their tiny apartment, nearly sixty-five years ago. Though she'd written the words herself, Belle felt her throat constrict, and warmth rush to her eyes.

And then her cell phone vibrated in her pocket.

She slipped it out discreetly and checked the number. It was her mother.

She clicked Ignore. In five minutes, Angelina would be finished. Belle could return the call then.

But in only two minutes her phone vibrated again. And again a minute later.

Finally, she felt the short buzz that meant a text message had come through.

In the applause that followed Angelina's final words, Belle pulled out the phone and read it.

Adam had another stroke.

He may not make it.
Meet me at hospital?

All the blood in Belle's body seemed to rush to her feet. How could this be? Everyone had been saying how much better Adam was. Belle had been so wrapped up in her own world, and so unsure how to progress beyond the roadblock of Joe's obvious rebuff, that she hadn't gone to see her new uncle at all.

But that didn't mean she didn't think about him, and care about him, and wish him health and happiness. In fact, she had been counting on having many years to work out all the complicated issues in the new family. She'd even dreamed that someday they'd have the kind of big happy mélange she envied in the Malone family.

Now…now it might be too late. Her uncle could die believing no one on her side of the family cared. Believing they were all like her dad.

Except for her mother. Her mother had been the only one to see that there was no time to waste.

Belle had to get there. She held her phone so tightly her damp palm heated the metal. She looked around the room for Matt.

She found him up by the dais, talking to Angelina and Brian Drayson, the business reporter from the *Chronicle*.

Without preamble, she touched his arm. "May I talk to you a minute?"

He smiled smoothly and excused himself without offering explanations. He took her to a quiet corner, his eyes quickly scanning her face and obviously seeing her emotions written there.

"What's wrong?"

"It's my uncle. He's had another stroke. I need to meet my mother at the hospital." Belle tried to think of a shorthand way to explain the nuances of the family dynamic. "It's a difficult situation. My father and my uncle are…estranged. My father thinks my mother is taking sides, and if he finds out she's there…"

But why was she going into so much detail? Matt didn't need to know. She'd seen his style of management. If an employee had a personal problem, Matt never asked questions. Time off was understood.

"Of course. Go ahead. Take as much time as you need. George can handle things here."

She nodded. "Thank you." She turned to go, but suddenly realized this hotel was fifteen miles out of town, away from the office, and she didn't have her own transportation.

She turned back. "I rode with George. We thought it would be more efficient, but—"

Matt didn't even bat an eye. "I'll take you."

"Oh, no. I can get a cab!" She was horrified. Why had she automatically brought this problem to him? Why hadn't she just found George in the first place? "I'll talk to George. You need to be here. Your grandmother, the reporters—"

"I'm just window dressing. George is far more useful here today than I am." Matt took her arm and began walking. "Come on. I have a very small, very silly car that I've never quite matured enough to trade in on something more sensible. But it has one advantage. It's fast. I can get you there in no time."

IT WAS INDEED A VERY fast car, not the sedan she remembered from the night of the Halloween party. He must have borrowed that one, or else he had several.

In fifteen minutes, she was at the hospital door, and five minutes later, after having thanked Matt profusely, she was hugging her mother in an ICU waiting room.

Sue was there, too, wearing sneakers and sweats, as if she'd been at the gym when she got the news. She was on her cell phone, probably making arrangements for the babies, but waved as Belle entered.

Joe Fraser stood alone near the window, looking grim and white-faced.

Belle crossed the underfurnished, boring beige room, which was probably supposed to be calming, but instead felt depressing. Maybe too many anxious families had sat here, paced here, stared out this same streaky window at the parking lot below.

"Joe, I'm so sorry," she said when she reached him. "How is your father? Have you heard anything?"

To her surprise, her mother followed her up to Joe and gently touched his forearm. He didn't pull away. In fact, he even mustered a smile and laid his hand over hers.

"They've stabilized him, but they don't sound reassuring," he said. "Apparently the next twenty-four hours are crucial."

"I'm sorry," Belle said again. It was not very useful, but it was all she had.

He wiped his free hand over his face, as if he needed to get the blood moving again, but it didn't improve his pallor. "Belle, this is a rotten time to talk about anything personal. But I want you to know I'm sorry about the things I said at lunch the other day."

Belle glanced toward her mother, wondering whether she was aware that Joe had once been so antagonistic about her visits. He certainly didn't seem antagonistic now. He still had his hand over Emily's, and it was clear the rapport between them hadn't been forged in the past fifteen minutes.

"Not that it's an excuse, but I've been…fighting on a lot of fronts lately. Adam and I— And my daughter—" He broke off. "Lots of things. Anyhow, trying to unkink the knots of this family mess…it was just one extra problem I didn't feel prepared to take on."

"You've done well," Emily said warmly. "You have been a rock for your father these past weeks, in spite of everything. You can rest easy on that score."

He squeezed Belle's mother's hand, and gave Belle another strained smile. "Luckily, Emily didn't let me push her away. She kept coming. And to tell the truth, it's been great knowing that, when I had to deal with some other drama, she could be here, looking after Adam for me."

Belle caught Sue's eye. Her cousin was still on the phone, but she must have been listening with one ear. She raised her brows, as if to say she was equally surprised.

How much time had her mother actually spent here, helping Adam recover, helping Joe struggle through? A lot, judging from Joe's emotional one-eighty.

No wonder her father was suspicious.

And no wonder Belle hadn't ever been able to find her mother alone, willing to have that long-overdue talk.

She was glad that her mom's generosity had found a grateful home. Glad that she'd been able to help Joe. And yet…it was unsettling to think that Emily had essentially been living a cloak-and-dagger existence for several weeks now. Belle wondered how often she herself had been used as an excuse, to keep her dad from finding out.

Was the overarching secret that Robert, Sarah and Jo had created so long ago, and all its complicated fallout, not morality lesson enough? Hadn't her mother seen how destructive secrets and lies could be?

Even as she formed the thought, Belle realized how hypocritical it was. With her secret investigation into Todd Kirkland, not to mention her continued pretense that she'd never met Matt Malone before, wasn't she guilty of similar sins?

Sue joined them, finally off the phone. "Where was Adam when it happened?"

"I don't know." Joe shook his head. "I've only been here about ten minutes myself. I was out of town on a job when the hospital called. And, well…it just didn't seem like one of the most important questions to ask."

"No, of course not." Emily seemed determined to keep Joe from feeling inadequate on any score. "It doesn't matter. He'll tell you himself, when he recovers."

"What about Daniel?" Sue looked worried, as if she didn't want Joe to have to cope with this alone.

Belle had met Daniel only once, briefly, the first time Adam had a stroke. Daniel was the only one of Joe Fraser's children who had been untouched by the Carson scandal—or the Carson blood. But, as Joe's uncle, he had apparently been a rock in Joe's life.

"Yes," Emily said, as if she knew all about the nuances of relationships in the Fraser circle. "What about Daniel? Can he come?"

"He's on his way," Joe said, and his expression lightened a bit. "He was even farther away than I was...he's been researching a new development in El Granada. Took me a while to reach him, but he's coming. Half an hour maybe? Maybe less."

Just then, the door to the waiting room opened, and all three of them jumped, proving how tightly their nerves were wound. Belle had been expecting either a doctor—*please, let it be good news*—or maybe even Daniel, who might have sped the whole way here.

But it was her father.

Sam Carson looked uncharacteristically disheveled. He wore his usual crisp khakis and expensive polo shirt, but his blond hair tumbled onto his forehead, and the knees of his slacks were grass-stained.

His movements were less precise than usual, too. He entered the waiting room with the half-focused gaze of someone who has just emerged from total darkness. He looked around the room blankly, as if he didn't recognize anyone in it.

And then, of course, it sank in.

"Emily?"

The word carried a world of disbelief...and dawning anger.

Belle took a step closer to her mother. Just in case.

But her mom didn't even flinch. She met her husband's gaze with surprising equanimity, as if she had known this moment would come, sooner or later, and had prepared herself for it.

"Sam." She neither welcomed him nor rejected him. She merely acknowledged him. "What are you doing here?"

"What am *I* doing here? That's hardly the question, is it? What the hell are *you* doing here?"

Joe stepped forward. "Emily is here because I asked her to come. Who invited you?"

"Watch your tone, son." Sam smoothed his hair out of his eyes and squared his shoulders. "I don't need your permission to be anywhere."

Belle recognized that low, snake-cold tone. It meant that Sam was precariously close to the edge. Close to losing his temper completely, an event that happened rarely and always left scorched earth behind.

"Dad, this isn't a time for bickering. Adam has had another stroke, and he—"

Her father's eyes cut briefly to her. "I know that. He was at my country club when it happened. Who do you think called the ambulance that brought him here?"

"Wait a minute." Joe's eyes narrowed. "He was with *you?*"

"Yes."

"What happened, Sam?" Joe took two steps toward her father, seemingly before he realized he was moving. "What did you do to him?"

"I didn't do a goddamn thing to him." Sam lowered his chin, and his square jaw and broad shoulders made him look like a bull about to charge. "I'll tell you one more time, son. Watch what you're saying."

"What did you do to him?"

"Nobody had to do anything to him." Sam's upper lip curled slightly. "I hear he checked himself out of the hospital the last time, against his doctor's advice. If your father is a sick man, he has no one to blame but himself."

Belle had seen her father intimidate many a man with that lowered head and razor-sharp eyes. Cowards were intimidated, and even brave men understood there was nothing to be gained by tangling with an ego freak.

Between the two, Sam had become used to prevailing.

But Belle could have told him that Joe, with his father possibly dying in the next room, was in no mood to be wise.

Joe took another step toward the older man, this one deliberate and provocative. "It can't be a coincidence that my father was with you when he had this stroke. I know damn well you did something, or said something. You're a toxic human being, Sam Carson, and I want you to get the hell out of here. Stay away from my family."

Sam smiled coldly. "*Your* family? I thought you Frasers were so goddamn proud of being Carsons. I thought the whole point was that the pathetic bastard lying in there is my *brother*."

Belle gasped, and so did Sue. But it was Emily who, out of nowhere, moved forward, her eyes blazing.

"You need to leave, Sam," she said emphatically. "Right now. You need to go home."

If her insubordination shocked him, he refused to show it. "I'll be glad to. And you'd better come with me, I think. You have a lot of explaining to do."

Emily took a breath. "No."

"No?" He frowned. "No what?"

"No, I'm not going home with you. No, I'm not explaining anything to you."

He hesitated a minute, and then tried to chuckle, as if he found her rebellion amusing. As if he considered her a child who might throw a tantrum from time to time and would have to be forgiven.

"Emily. Get hold of yourself. Don't be ridiculous."

"Mom," Belle said, as confused as her dad was by this new, self-contained woman who didn't seem to care what Sam Carson wanted. "I can stay. Sue's here, and Daniel will be arriving any minute. If you want to—"

"But I don't want to." Her mother turned and faced Belle, her eyes sad but not terrified, not meek, not red-rimmed or struggling to hold back tears. "I probably should have done this years ago, back when I could have saved you, too. But I'm leaving him. I had already decided, even before this shameless display of…cruelty."

She looked back at her husband. "I'm sorry, Sam. I have no intention of ever going home again."

AN HOUR LATER, Belle let the elevator lower her slowly to the lobby. Her mind was numb. She'd never been so emotionally drained in her entire life.

The news about Adam wasn't great. Her heart felt bruised, aching for the opportunities lost.

After Emily's announcement, Sam had left immediately. Sue and Emily had both left shortly after that, though they'd promised to return as soon as they could. Sue needed to coordinate care for the babies. And Emily had been picked up by a friend from the museum board, a middle-aged widower who had offered her his guest room until she got a place of her own.

A male friend. Not a boyfriend, she'd assured Belle with a sad smile. Though of course Sam would probably paint it that way. Belle had tried to smile back.

Belle had stayed with Joe until Daniel arrived. Her cousin had apologized several times for causing a problem between Emily and Sam, but she'd assured him he wasn't to blame. This storm had been building for years.

When she was a little girl, she used to fantasize about her mother bursting into her bedroom, two suitcases in hand, saying, "Hurry! We're running away to Italy."

Belle always picked that destination because of the boot-shaped birthmark on her hip. It was, she supposed, her version of believing she was secretly a princess kidnapped by the Gypsies, someday to be returned to her rightful throne.

But now that her mother's flight had finally become reality...

Why did it leave her with such a hollow feeling in the pit of her stomach? Paradoxically, it was the thought of her father that made her the most uncomfortable. Through the years, from all she could tell, he'd had a succession of "liaisons," mostly with ambitious saleswomen who wanted to rise through the ranks faster than any business acumen could take them, but he didn't have any real friends.

Her mother would probably, in the end, be fine. She was still beautiful, and she might find someone to give all that unwanted love to. Or she might just thrive on being independent.

But Belle's dad…

What would become of him? He had no real intimates. No one to talk to. No one to help him come to terms with what had happened.

No one to teach him how to win back his wife.

When Belle reached the quiet lobby, she pulled out her cell phone. She'd call a cab and get home somehow. It wasn't quite dark yet, but she was already exhausted. Maybe, after a long night's sleep, things wouldn't look so grim.

But before she could find the cab company in her cell's phone book, she saw Matt Malone standing by the front door. He smiled as she approached.

"How's your uncle?"

"They can't really tell yet." Her brain didn't feel as if it was working very well. She couldn't figure out why he was here. "Have you been… Did you wait for me?"

"I wanted to be sure you had a ride home."

"Oh, no. You didn't have to do that."

"Of course I did." He tilted his head. "Did you think I'd just leave you here?"

For some reason, though she'd kept her composure through all the drama upstairs, through the disintegration of her family right before her eyes, this simple question suddenly made her eyes fill with tears.

"Belle." He put his arm around her, and the safe warmth of him flooded through her chest. It felt good in a prickling, painful way, as if it began to thaw the stiff pride she'd been using to hold herself together.

"Come on," he said softly. "We need to get you home."

CHAPTER THIRTEEN

HE SHOULD HAVE CALLED her a cab. He should have phoned George to take her home.

Hell, he should have given her his sports car, title and all, and hitchhiked home, if necessary. He had another car.

He should have done whatever it took to keep himself away from her.

But he was a selfish bastard, and he didn't do it. Instead, he bundled her into his car and drove her home.

He tried to persuade himself that he would just drop her off at the door. That he wouldn't go in, on the pretext of making sure she was okay. That he wouldn't take her in his arms and try to love away whatever was hurting her so much.

If he did any of that, it would be indefensible. She was vulnerable, undone by whatever had happened in the hospital. She tried to hide it, but she was crying. His car was too small for privacy, and he was aware of every unnatural hitch and subtle quiver in her breathing, aware of the silent tears that slid in glittering trails down her cheeks. Belle was so close he could lean over and kiss them away, almost without taking his eye off the road.

And he was burning up with the desire to do exactly that.

When one of her sobs reached an audible level, he couldn't stand it anymore. He reached out and took her hand, which she had clenched in her lap.

She didn't resist. Instead, she clung to him. It wasn't personal, really. It seemed instinctive, as if she wanted him to tether her, wanted him to keep the emotions from sweeping her off, the way the bowlines in the boathouse kept the currents from tugging the *Mac-Gregor* out into open seas.

He felt the heat of her thigh against the back of his hand.

He pressed his foot harder on the gas, hoping he'd reach her apartment before his willpower was completely burned away.

As if holding his hand did help, her tears slowed and finally stopped.

She began to tell him about the domestic roller-coaster ride she'd been on for the past few months. The discovery of her grandfather's double life, and the secret family that had always been living beside them, on the other side of the looking glass. The tensions, her new uncle's stroke, the rupture between her mom and dad.

No wonder she had to let off some steam in the form of a few tears. It was a miracle any of the Carsons, right side of the blanket or wrong, could function right now.

She seemed calmer after she'd talked about it. But she didn't let go of his hand.

A few minutes later, he found the address she'd given him. It was in a modest section of Noe Valley, a bank of town houses very similar to the ones where

Diamante was located, except without the corporate gloss. Similar rentals were sprinkled all over the older neighborhoods of San Francisco, where people were willing to trade space for charm. He knew without seeing it that her apartment would be small but beautiful, with wooden floors that creaked and elegant crown molding whose detail had been blurred by too many decades of paint.

He knew because he'd lived in one, in his first couple of years after college.

For several seconds after he parked the car, she didn't speak, just looked out the window at the town house. She didn't even seem to remember she was holding his hand, which was fine with him. He reached across the steering wheel and turned the key with his left hand, reluctant to let the moment end.

"Thank you for waiting for me," she said. It was growing dusky, but he could still see that her eyes were a little swollen, and rimmed with a hint of red, which only made them look bluer than ever. "And for listening."

"It was nothing. I'm glad you were willing to talk. I wish there was something I could do."

She bit her lower lip and, shifting, ended up leaning toward him just a little. He smelled the perfume he'd learned so well. Passing car lights spotlighted the yellow curls that tickled her graceful, ivory neck.

He glanced down. Suddenly, the way their naked fingers were braided together, skin to skin, seemed unbearably intimate, even sexual.

He had to take a deep breath, to bank the fire that was building.

"Matt...I..." She tried to smile. "Would you like to come in?"

Yes, his body said. His fingertips twitched. He gritted his teeth against the sudden fiery pain.

"That probably isn't the best idea," he forced himself to say.

"Please. I'd like to thank you. I don't have any wine, but I could make some coffee."

"No. Thanks." His voice didn't sound right. It sounded husky and almost angry. He wasn't angry. It just took extra force to make the words come out. "It's probably better if I go."

Another car's headlights revealed the tiny frown line between her eyes. "Why? I'm finished being weepy, I promise. I won't—"

"No, damn it," he said gruffly. "That's not why. I *want* to come in. God knows I want it so badly I'm about to lose my mind. But surely you know what will happen if I do."

She looked down at their hands, still entwined in her lap. And then she looked back at him. "You'll make love to me."

"Yes," he said. "I will make love to you. I won't be able to help myself. Frankly, the only thing that's stopping me right now is that stupid gearshift on the floor between us."

"Then come in," she said. "Please. Come in. There's no reason why you shouldn't."

He groaned softly. "There's every reason in the world. You're hurting right now. I don't want to take advantage—"

"Yes, I'm hurting." Her voice was surprisingly firm. "But only because I've seen what can happen when people waste years, afraid to be honest about what they feel and what they want. Only because I've seen how you can live your whole life preparing for tomorrow, but then it's too late. Tomorrow doesn't come."

He wanted to believe it. Every nerve ending he possessed was screaming at him, telling him to shut up, to stop arguing. He had the "yes" he'd been dreaming about, and he should take it while he could.

"Belle, all the rules say no. My job…your job…"

She smiled. "If that's the problem, I quit. Tonight I won't be your employee, and you won't be my boss. You can hire me back tomorrow if you want. If you don't, I don't care."

She raised their hands to her heart. It was beating hard, almost too fast to believe. "I want this, Matt. I want it more than I have ever wanted anything. Please. Come upstairs with me."

In the end, he wasn't strong enough. It was as simple as that.

He nodded.

She let go of his hand, finally, and opened her car door.

He opened his, too, welcoming the brisk San Francisco air that blew in on him. He stood, still throbbing from head to toe with longing, and followed her up the small flight of stairs to her door.

As he watched her put the key in the lock, he forced himself to be honest, to look past the easy delusion of sensual witchery. He was making a mistake, a big mistake, and it was no one's fault but his own.

He wasn't drunk, or hypnotized or tempted beyond sanity. He was going to take what Belle Carson offered him because he wanted it. Pure and simple. He wanted it, he wanted her, and he couldn't bear the thought of leaving here tonight, only to endure another eight years of regret.

Maybe he was doing it for the same reason she was doing it. Because he'd seen what happened when you let a chance at happiness pass you by.

Soundlessly, the door opened. The interior was dark. Her face was a pale, heart-shaped ghost against the blackness.

"Matt?" Her voice trembled. "Please…"

He joined her in the shadows, shutting the door behind them. Shutting out reality. Instantly they were plunged into a silver-black half world, where he was a stranger, she was a mystery and the rules no longer applied.

He pulled her into his arms without a word, groaning with relief as his hands roamed over her body with a license he would never have permitted himself out there in the real world, where he wasn't allowed to touch her.

She was hot and trembling, and her hands were moving, too. She traced her palms, her fingertips, her lips, across his face, as if she wanted to learn his shape and contours, learn him in ways vision alone could never allow.

Their panting breaths were the only sound in this twilight world, and moonbeams filtered through a leafy maple were the only illumination. He recognized nothing. A twinkle on the wall might have been the frame of a picture, and the glimmer off to the right might have been the chrome on a kitchen appliance.

Or it could all have been magic.

He unbuttoned her shirt, his fingers flying, driven by the need to feel the high, hard thrust of her breasts against his palms. The shirt fell to the floor, skimming past his own bare chest, and he realized that she had unbuttoned his shirt, too.

He shrugged it away from his arms, and then he pulled her in, unable to get her close enough. Her nipples were tight, creating flashes of heat where they pressed into his skin. He kissed her neck, her collarbone, her breasts, and then he couldn't wait any longer.

Sinking to his knees, he unzipped her skirt and pushed it to the floor, as well. She stepped out of it gracefully, groaning softly as he buried his face in the lace of her panties. He reached up and hooked one finger through each side of the flimsy elastic that held the two scraps of fabric together.

She put her hands on his head, tunneling her fingers through his hair, as he slid the panties down, slowly, exposing inch after inch of skin, trailing kisses until he felt the warm tickle of blond silk between her legs.

"Matt," she whispered, a ghost voice in the darkness.

He didn't answer. His mouth was busy, opening her gently, searching for the secret nub at the core of her. A tremor passed through her thighs as his lips closed over it. He tasted her, the intensely female, salty sweetness of her, and felt his penis pressing at the confines of his jeans, answering the primitive call of that scent.

She was damp. Warm. Ready. He tugged softly with his tongue, then released, then tugged again, making her harden, and swell, and throb to his guided rhythm.

She called out, more a noise than a name, and he increased the tempo. Tug and release, tug and release, until her fingers tightened in his hair and her thighs trembled under his hands.

She arched back, gave a half-strangled cry. Her whole body seemed to quake and shudder, and then collapse into his waiting arms.

He picked her up, and carried her through the door that he knew must lead to the bedroom. In here, a streetlight picked up sparkles and glitters on every surface…a mirror, a silver hairbrush, a crystal decanter, something on the wall, something in the closet.

He would make her sparkle, too. He would give her a night to remember.

He laid her on the bed. She was loose-limbed, but still breathing shallowly, and her hands reached for his belt buckle, one last glimmer in the enchanted midnight. Together, they removed the jeans, and the boxers beneath. He always kept a condom—one benefit of his former life with a series of temporary Tiffanis was that taking risks was out of the question.

And then the waiting was finally over. He entered her with a strange sense of joy he couldn't remember ever feeling before. She was beautiful, her body receptive….

But it was more than that.

He filled her slowly, savoring the rightness, the perfect fit, the warm, fluid ecstasy. The sense of completion, as if he'd found the part of himself that he hadn't even realized was missing.

She was smiling, and her eyes were glistening, as if they still held tears. He touched her cheek.

"No," she said. "I'm happy, Matt. Make love to me."

His body took over then, only too willing to obey. Keeping his eyes locked on hers, he began to move, slowly at first, hunting for the rhythm and depth and force that would take them to the edge and keep them there forever.

She rose to meet him, and her body spoke to his, asking for more. Her legs wrapped around his back, pulling him in, and he kept answering, giving her anything she wanted. He flirted with the razor edge of the release, driving perilously close, then pulling back.

But suddenly, somewhere in that dangerous game, he realized with a momentary sense of panic that, for the first time in his memory, he wasn't in control anymore.

With the scent of her filling his lungs, and the satin of her skin sweating beneath his hands, the sensations were stronger than he was.

This wasn't a climax he could toy with like a yo-yo, reeling it in and out in some kind of torturous, sensual sport.

It was an earthquake moving through him.

He called her name, as if she could save him, even though he could hardly see her anymore.

She wrapped her arms around him, holding him together as he shuddered, arched and fought the beautiful pain. And when he collapsed against her, lost and exhausted, she stroked his damp brow.

He tried to breathe. Tried to find the strength in his muscles. He waited for the conflagration's smoke to clear from his brain.

He rolled to the side, afraid he would hurt her. She curled up under his arm and, still smiling, went to sleep.

He blinked, dazed and drained, trying to figure out what had just happened to him. Trying to understand why making love to Belle Carson was so different from anything he'd ever done in his life.

And so terrifying.

He stared, only half seeing, at the small spot of crystalline sparkle on the wall beside her dresser, wondering idly what it was. It seemed important somehow....

But how? He couldn't follow any of his thoughts through to an answer. Car lights moved across the spot on the wall, making the crystal glimmer on, then off, then on again.

It was like watching the chain swung by a hypnotist.

His eyelids grew heavy. A few more sleepy blinks, and the crystal, the room itself, and even Belle beside him, disappeared into the mist.

CHAPTER FOURTEEN

BELLE AWOKE TO THE sound of the doorbell ringing.

And ringing, and ringing.

It took a minute to remember where she was. And with whom.

And...her skin shivered deliciously...*why*.

Matt was sound asleep beside her, the sheet tugged across his hips, his strong, dark legs bare and disturbingly sensual.

She squinted at her watch. Though the apartment was in pitch darkness, it was only about nine-thirty. She thought, her brain still oddly muddled, that it might be Pandora at the door. Or maybe even her mother.

Belle tried to remember how many articles of clothing she and Matt had left on the living room floor.

She grabbed a robe from the closet, slinging it on while she quietly shut the bedroom door. Then she rushed around, scooping up slips and skirts and panties as she darted through the room.

In the split second before she opened the front door, she faced the fact that it might be her father.

Well, too bad. She hadn't ever chosen her mother's peacekeeper tactics. Belle hadn't ever ducked a fight when her father insisted on one. If he dared to comment on her love life, she would be glad to explain just exactly how much it wasn't his business.

She opened the door before the bell could ring again. She'd be glad to go toe-to-toe with her dad in the entry, but she didn't want Matt to wake up.

But of course, because nothing was ever that simple, it wasn't her dad.

It was David. He looked on edge, almost angry, though David didn't ordinarily do anger. It had been one of his biggest selling points.

"God, Belle, I've been trying to get you for hours. Why aren't you answering your cell?"

She tried to remember…. She'd switched it off when she got to the hospital. She had meant to turn it back on to check for the cab company's phone number, but then Matt had appeared.

"I guess I left it off," she said, adjusting the collar on her robe awkwardly. The brand label appeared to be on the outside. "But what's so urgent? Is something wrong?"

"Yes, something's wrong!" He ran his hand through his hair. "It's my client, the one who wants to sue Diamante. He's missing. He's been depressed lately, and his wife is really worried. She's afraid he might be going after Malone himself."

"Surely not," Belle breathed. "That would be insane."

David grimaced. "Desperate people do insane things. Look, Belle, I need to know if you've found anything on Todd Kirkland. You haven't answered my e-mails. I don't know whether you've been able to unearth anything about the fund. If you have, I need to know. If we find him, it might help him to know we're making progress."

"I haven't," she said, flushing. "I'm sorry. It's been busy, and I—"

"Damn it." David looked crestfallen. "Can I come in? I want to call his wife, but I don't want to talk out here—"

"It's not really a good time," she began.

David finally seemed to see past his own distress and to assimilate what he was looking at. She tried to picture it: a dark apartment, a woman with wild hair, makeup kissed completely off, a robe tossed on inside out...standing ankle deep in discarded clothes, some of them obviously male.

"You're—you're with someone?"

"David, I'm sorry," she repeated.

She didn't know what else to say. She wouldn't have had him stumble into this for anything in the world. She would have died rather than hurt him again. But she didn't want to discuss this now.

And then, behind her, she heard the sound her subconscious had been dreading since the moment she saw David Gerard standing on her front stoop.

The sound of her bedroom door opening.

David's eyes moved toward the noise. After a split second's confusion, they widened. His mouth opened and hung there.

And that was the end of her last hope, the off chance he didn't know what Matt Malone looked like.

"Jesus, Belle," David said bitterly.

She glanced over her shoulder, hugging the crumpled clothes to her pounding heart with her left hand. Matt stood in the doorway, casually leaning against the jamb. He wore only his jeans, feet and torso bare. In his hands he was holding…

He was holding the framed earring.

Her heart was about to explode. She couldn't see how any of this could end well, but she had to try. "David, look, I'm sorry, but I just can't talk about this now—"

"Yeah, my showing up while His Highness is still here is quite the inconvenience, isn't it?"

"Listen. Please. David."

He shook his head, almost inarticulate with a fury she'd thought he didn't possess. "You've been *busy?* Sorry, Belle, but what you've been is seduced. You've been *had.* This son of a bitch has charmed you right out of your clothes *and* your ethics. You haven't had *time* to investigate Todd Kirkland? What a crock!"

Flinching, she glanced over her shoulder again, knowing that Matt had heard every syllable. Especially the damning words *Todd Kirkland.*

Matt's head was tilted, making him look slightly bemused. But it was an act, because his eyes had the merciless, stone-cold stare of an executioner.

He looked at her, then at David, and then once more at the little framed box he held in his hand.

"Matt, I…"

Slowly, he smiled. It didn't look like any smile she'd ever seen on his face before. It put even her father's sardonic grins to shame.

And then he started to laugh.

"What's so funny, Malone?" David's fair face was reddening. He was a smart man. He knew that laugh had nothing to do with humor, and everything to do with contempt.

He just didn't understand that the contempt wasn't directed at him. It was directed at Belle.

"Matt," she began again, her heart racing. Then she uttered the three little words that had been the death of so many relationships. "I can explain."

"No, really," Matt said, letting the laughter die off to a bitter chuckle. "There's no need. I've been a fool for a long time now, but I think I'm finally wising up."

"You don't understand—"

"Of course I do. It was brilliantly done, Belle." He came over to the door, and handed the framed earring to her. When she couldn't raise her free hand to take it, he raised it for her and placed the box firmly against her palm, wrapping her fingers around it.

"I think my only question is whether you've hated me ever since that night. Did it injure your pride, my falling asleep? Have you been waiting ever since for an opportunity to extract a little cold revenge?"

"What the hell are you talking about?" David moved into the room, as if, in spite of everything, he couldn't stand by and allow someone to speak harshly to Belle.

But Matt ignored him as completely as if he'd been invisible, like a gnat that didn't even buzz on his frequency. Matt plucked his shirt from the floor and began shrugging it on, his face thoughtful.

"Or was it simply coincidence that taking a job with me gave you a chance to reinstate yourself as an investigative journalist? Or…maybe the simplest explanation is the best. Maybe everything is a charade with you."

"You're wrong," she said. "So wrong."

"No, I'm your classic horny male moron, but I'm not wrong." He reached out and touched her face. "It's okay, little Cleo. A lot of people get a thrill out of pretending to be something they're not. And how nice that, this time, I could get a thrill out of it, too."

TWO WEEKS LATER, on the Friday before the last of Diamante's beach events, Belle read a news brief in the paper reporting that Todd Kirkland had resigned as manager of Diamante's Drivers Fund.

The newspaper had no details, apparently accepting at face value Kirkland's statement that he needed to spend more time with his wife, who had recently been diagnosed with breast cancer. The article didn't even hint, in that time-honored way journalists had of suggesting something they weren't legally able to say straight out, that there had been any monkey business with the fund.

Still, she wanted to know the truth.

Calling Diamante was obviously not possible. She hadn't heard from Matt since the night David came to her door, bringing his tale of betrayal that was almost true. Just true enough to hang her.

After that disastrous night, she hadn't needed to hear that she was fired. She'd simply called George and thanked him for giving her a chance at Diamante, saying it wasn't going to work out. He'd wanted to know more, of course, but she'd kept it short and sweet.

She couldn't even ask George what had happened with Kirkland, not unless she was ready to volunteer information of her own in return.

So she went to the only place she could think of.

She went to David Gerard.

She arrived at his office just before five, when she knew he'd be finished with clients, and settling in for the quiet work: research, brief-writing, correspondence. Amanda, his paralegal, looked a little nervous, but waved Belle through, probably hoping she had arrived for a reconciliation.

Amanda and Belle had been friends.

As Belle entered, David looked up from his computer. He didn't smile.

"Sorry to bother you," she said. She didn't take a chair, and he didn't offer one.

"I thought you might call." He tapped the newspaper folded on the right corner of his desk, as always. He kept a neat office, just as he'd always kept a neat apartment. "When the article ran, I mean. I didn't think you'd actually make the trip."

She smiled. "I wasn't sure you wouldn't hang up on me."

He tapped his pencil against his keyboard a minute, then sighed, dropped it and swiveled to face her. "I wouldn't have," he said. "Sit down. We aren't enemies."

She sat. His chair was comfortable and expensive, and familiar. She'd sat here a hundred times, waiting for him to finish up some work before they rode home together.

It seemed like a lifetime ago.

"I'm sorry, David. I did try to get you some information, but I just couldn't bring myself to follow through. And about Matt…well…I'm sorry about that, too. I wouldn't have wanted you to find out in such an awkward way."

"No, you don't have to apologize," he said. "I've been thinking it through. I overreacted that night. I don't sleep in your bed anymore, and I have no right to judge who does. And you never promised me anything about Kirkland, either. I was just…disappointed."

"Thanks," she said. "I appreciate it."

He looked uncomfortable, as if he was well aware they'd only skimmed the surface of what had happened that night. For one thing, he'd always wondered why she kept that framed earring, and he was probably dying of curiosity now, though he'd never admit it.

She would have told him, but it was such a ridiculous, embarrassing story. And it still hurt too much even to think about it. She'd put the earring in her bedroom wastebasket that night, but like a fool had taken it out again in the morning. She'd settled for burying it at the bottom of her winter underwear drawer.

"I hear you've left Diamante, too." David was somber. "I'm sorry. I feel as if that's my fault. I shouldn't have mentioned Kirkland. It was a stupid slip."

She looked at him with a small smile, but didn't say anything.

"Okay," he said, cracking as easily as he always had. He was a terrible liar, and worked scrupulously hard to be honest, even to himself, about himself. "I know it wasn't a slip. I was stung, seeing another man come walking out of that bedroom. I wanted to sting back."

It took courage to be that direct. She admired that, and so much else about him. He really was a very nice man.

But now that she'd discovered what real love felt like, she was astonished that she'd ever believed she could make a life out of even the warmest admiration. She'd been wrong to try. It had encouraged him to hope, and that had been selfish.

"It's okay," she said. "I put myself in that position, and I got what I deserved. I should never have agreed to look into Kirkland in the first place. Matt was right. I was trying to have it both ways…paying the rent with his job while I tried to worm my way back into the newspaper business. It was crummy. I was a fool to do it."

David shrugged. Clearly he still didn't like to hear anyone criticize her…even Belle herself. "So I guess you want to know what happened? With Kirkland, I mean?"

"Yeah. Whatever you're free to tell."

"Honestly, I don't know much, not for a fact. I suspect plenty, but here's what I know. My client, who came home safely at dawn that night, by the way, drunk as a skunk but in one piece, has decided not to sue. I met with Diamante's lawyer, coincidently another guy named Malone."

"That would be Colby."

David smiled. "Yeah. Well, I'm not on a first-name basis, like you are. But I met with the guy, who seems pretty straight up. He wanted all the information, and he opened the discussion by offering my client—" David paused and raised his eyebrows "—what we lawyers call a sizable sum."

"A pay-off?"

"I don't know. Somehow I don't really think so. No one admitted it, but if you ask me, they looked into this Kirkland bastard on their own, and probably found all kinds of irregularities in the fund. My client tells me that several of his friends, other drivers whose requests for aid had been turned down, have been compensated in the past couple of weeks."

David opened his hands. "Next thing I hear, Lawyer Malone calls to tell me Todd Kirkland has decided to retire. Lawyer talk for he's guilty as sin, but now that we've gelded him, we're letting him go because he's a family friend."

Belle nodded. Sounded about right. "So, in the end, you got justice, which is even better than winning a case, right?"

He nodded in turn.

"What are you planning to do now?"

David laughed. "I'm going to take a vacation. I'm thinking Bermuda, not that I can afford it, since I waived my usual percentage of this guy's settlement. Still, I hear there are all kinds of hot chicks in Bermuda."

Belle stood, appreciating his attempt to make her feel better. She'd definitely celebrate the day he found someone new to love.

"Thanks," she said. "Have fun on your trip. The ladies are always drooling over you. You just have to notice them."

"That might be easier to do in Bermuda. Around here they're a bit eclipsed, if you know what I mean."

Smiling to acknowledge the compliment, she headed for the door. She knew what he meant, but she also knew he'd get over it.

Just as she would have to get over Matt Malone.

Somehow.

"Oh, and Belle?"

She turned. David had a sheepish smile on his face.

It made him look more gorgeous than ever. But nothing inside her shifted. In her heart, a dark and sardonic face shut out everything else. "What?"

"When I get back, I was thinking. If you're still interested, I might be in the market for a friend."

As long as she was on the world tour of difficult visits, Belle decided to drive out to see her father.

She'd left several messages for him in the past couple of weeks, but he'd ignored them all. Her mother, on the other hand, had been eager to spend time together.

It was true, apparently, that misery loved company. Both of them were brokenhearted, and both pretending not to be. At first they tried denial. They shopped and dined out, bought dueling pedicures, apartment hunted on the Internet and even repainted Belle's bedroom.

Then they tried wallowing. They watched three-hanky movies till Belle's glasses fogged up. They nicknamed Belle's apartment Heartbreak Hotel. And, just to rub salt into the wound, they ordered Cinnamon Diamonds from the nearest Diamante Pizza.

Belle's streak of rotten luck held. She kept untwisting the pastries long after she was too full to eat another bite. Her lips and fingers were covered in sticky white frosting, but she didn't find a single ring inside.

Today, they'd decided to put the self-pity party on hold…perhaps permanently. Belle's mother had a museum board meeting in the afternoon, followed by dinner at a friend's house. They both knew it was time to put away the hankies and venture back into the real world.

They'd both been several times to see Adam, who was stable, but not quite out of the woods. He still had some speech impairment, and some one-sided paralysis. It would be quite a while, the doctors said, before they could be sure how far his recovery would take him.

But Joe and Sue were with Adam today. So Belle was on her own. She'd already taken her dose of contrition and humility with David. Maybe that put her in the right mind-set for checking in on her dad.

The sun was setting as she arrived, and his silver SUV glowed with a peach-colored light. The bricks that led up to the kitchen door shone, too, as if they'd been lit up in welcome.

Her mother's tub of begonias spilled over with a hundred blossoms. The ivy creeper fluttered in the breeze.

On the outside, nothing had changed.

But the minute Belle opened the kitchen door and heard the silence, she knew. It was so quiet she could hear the drone of the refrigerator as it cycled through another tray of ice. The air was chilled and stale, as if no one lived here anymore.

"Dad?"

No answer. She put her purse on the kitchen island, next to her mother's bowl of knitting yarn, and moved into the house. "Dad?"

From the doorway of the TV room, pale gray and blue shadows played on the tile, shifting and blinking like underwater ghosts. She turned in that direction. He must be watching TV. Maybe with his earphones on he couldn't hear her call.

A habit he likely found hard to break, even though

there was no one else in the house now who could be bothered by his noise.

He had his back to her, but she could tell by his stance that he was practicing putting. The TV was tuned to the news, on mute, which automatically displayed closed captions on the screen: "…and do you really think it's going to stay this nice all summer, Jim? Not likely, Andrea. You know what Mark Twain said about a summer in San Francisco…."

"Dad?"

He must have had the sound quite loud, because he still didn't respond. He was scowling at his putter as if the only ingredient necessary to sink the ball was sheer mental intensity.

He took a practice swing or two, each no wider than eighteen inches, and then hit the ball. It landed in the mechanical cup, which lit up and then spat the ball back at him again.

This could go on all night.

She touched his shoulder. "Dad?"

He looked up, flinching. When he saw who it was, he didn't appear furious, as she'd feared he might, but he didn't look thrilled, either. You would have thought that playing golf by himself in an empty house, listening to talking heads patter about the weather, piped straight into his brain by a pair of high-tech earbuds, was the most scintillating activity a man could wish for.

"Hello, Isabelle," he said. He tugged one earphone out and let it dangle. "If you've come to apologize, I'm afraid it's a bit too late."

No, she thought. She hadn't come to apologize, because she hadn't done anything wrong.

But she didn't say it. New rules. He could bait, but she didn't have to bite.

"I've just come to see if you're okay. I'm worried about you, Dad. How've you been…since Mom left?"'

He lined up another putt. "I've been fine. I'm not sure what you expected. Did you think I would starve to death? I do know how to cook, you know."

"Of course." But that kitchen hadn't been touched since her mother left, and they both knew it. "I guess I thought you might be lonely."

He scoffed. "Why? What's different? It's not as if she was showering me with TLC day and night. I'd hardly seen her for weeks." He hit the ball and missed. "I guess now we know why."

Belle let that go, too. It got easier, each time she passed up a chance to pick a fight.

"Have you heard from her?" She knew he hadn't. "Has she called?"

He shook his head. His jaw tightened.

"Well," she said, trying not to grow impatient, though he clearly wasn't getting the point. "Have you tried to call her?"

He looked up. "Why would I do that?"

She dropped onto the arm of the sofa, letting out a sigh. "You want her to come home, don't you?"

He didn't answer. But that was answer enough.

"She's not going to just wake up one morning and decide to come crawling back, Dad. You're going to have to talk to her. You're going to have to meet her halfway."

"Halfway to her boyfriend's house?" He shifted his shoulders, squaring off for another putt. "Don't hold your breath."

Belle practically had to bite her tongue to keep from pointing out that the friend with the spare room was not a boyfriend. And that, if they wanted to start talking adultery, they'd have to go a long way back, all the way to Sam's first assistant, a curvy number named Nell.

But Belle had promised herself that she'd be restrained…that she'd say only positive, constructive things that might help him figure out how to rebuild these exploded bridges.

He cleared his throat. "I guess you think it's fine, what she did. Going behind my back…"

"Not really." Belle tried to sound neutral. "I think seeing Adam was fine. He's family, and she thought he needed her. But doing it behind your back was a mistake."

"It damn sure was."

"Yes. You'd think, after everything that's happened, no Carson would dream of keeping a secret that could blow up in our faces at any moment." She sighed, lamenting her own stupid secrets. She was no better than the rest of them.

"And yet," she finished heavily, "somehow we just keep doing it."

"I don't." He picked up the golf ball and rolled it absently through his fingers. "People may think I'm abrasive, but at least I tell it like it is. I don't have any secrets."

Belle smiled. "Of course you do, Dad."

"I do not." He narrowed his eyes. "I know you've

always believed that I played around on your mother. And there may have been a time…"

He trailed off, looking less certain of himself than she'd ever seen him. The blue shadows moved across his shirt, his shoulder, even, weirdly, the side of his cheek. He pulled the other earbud out, as if he needed to think, and the noise was interfering.

"But not anymore, Belle. Not for a long time."

"I'm glad," she said, and she was, deeply. If that was true, perhaps her parents' marriage still had a chance.

"But I think you have an even more profound secret than that. One that, if you don't share it with Mom, could permanently mess up both your lives."

"Oh, really?" He set his lips, as if he found it ridiculous that Belle would dare to try to instruct him about anything. "And what might that secret be?"

She smiled, hearing the fear behind the bravado. She reached out to touch her father's hand. He stiffened, but didn't pull away.

"That you love her, of course. That you miss her. That you want her to come home."

CHAPTER FIFTEEN

MATT WAS SO *OVER* THIS pizza-on-the-beach thing.

Thank God this was the last one. Once upon a time, it had seemed like a great idea. Okay, it still was a great idea. The word of mouth was amazing, and the new franchises were off to great starts.

But without Belle…

It wasn't the same. He didn't feel any of the things he was supposed to be projecting. He didn't feel inspired, energized or even remotely charismatic.

He just felt hot, uncomfortable, bored and ridiculous.

George nudged his elbow. "Smile, boss," he whispered. "Remember the mantra. 'Having fun, pizzas in the sun. Next reporter shows up at one.'"

"Shut up, George," Matt muttered. That joke had been mildly funny four hours ago, but it was more like five o'clock now. He'd talked to a dozen reporters since that first microphone had been stuck in his face at one on the dot.

But he knew his PR director was right, so he stood a little straighter, slapping the "having a blast" grin back on his face.

Just another hour. Just till six o'clock, and then he could get the hell out of here.

Off to his left, the WWHM truck blocked his view of the water, and the ever-delightful Andy in the Afternoon kept a running commentary for his listeners, ringing a merciless six-foot cowbell every time a customer found one of the hidden rings in a Cinnamon Diamond.

Obviously recognizing that people eager to win a diamond solitaire might include a lot of ladies also eager to get married, a local bridal store had decided to pair up with the promotion. They were giving away a free rhinestone tiara to the first ten ladies who found rings today. It had been a real boost to business, but…

Who would have thought gorgeous women in bikinis were so hot for tiaras?

And who would have thought that Matt would be so completely bored by looking at an endless line of them, queuing up to buy Cinnamon Diamonds and flirt a little with Diamante's sunburned CEO?

Red would have had something philosophical to say about the lust for little sparkling crowns. He had broken up with Marie after the night of the gold chain discussion, and hadn't taken on a new girlfriend yet.

"They're all the same," he'd said plaintively. "You just know they're looking at your gold fillings, thinking how they'd make a darling pair of earrings."

Matt checked his watch. Forty-five minutes.

If only Andy in the Afternoon wasn't watching like Big Brother from the van, telling the whole damn world what Matt Malone was up to. He might have slipped away early.

Instead, with George pinning him down on one side, and Andy on the other, Matt had to pretend that this bleached blonde in front him, with a bathing suit made out of what appeared to be three Post-it notes, was as adorable as she thought she was.

He knew, without touching it, that her hair would feel like straw, and her breasts would be about as sexy as giant marbles. She was laughing, presumably at something he'd said, though he knew for a fact he wasn't that funny, and the sound grated on his ears.

One night had changed everything.

No, just three hours, that was all he and Belle had had, really....

Three hours of a real woman, made of soft, simple parts, warm curves and silky curls. Three hours, and he was ruined for everything else.

Brilliant, Malone. You've really made a mess of it now.

Finally, the blonde took her pizza and reluctantly moved to the next line to receive her free Cinnamon Diamonds.

"If I win a ring, I want you to put it on my finger," she called back to Matt merrily. "Okay?"

"You bet," he answered, laughing. Playing the game he used to love to play.

And then he saw her.

Belle Carson stood in his pizza line, watching him flirt with the blonde. Three people back, behind two more bathing beauties and a little girl with fat silver braces and a fiendish scowl.

His heart just plain stopped. He had a pizza box in his hand, and he held it out there, frozen like a mannequin.

What was she doing here?

She wore something blue, a material so light it fluttered around her knees. Her shoulders were bare, but she'd brought a sweater, as if she had learned her lesson the last time. Her hair was loose, spinning in the wind.

George saw her, too.

"Don't," he said under his breath. "Don't give the radio guy anything to work with. He might recognize her as a former employee. And you know the Kirkland story could rise from the dead any minute."

Matt flicked a glance at George. "I'm not a fool," he said.

He had plenty to say to Belle Carson, but he didn't intend to let it all end up on the six o'clock news.

With effort, he pulled himself together and sold pizza to the three people in front of her with enough charm to please even the most demanding PR taskmaster. One of them found a ring in a cinnamon roll, though thank God it wasn't the bleached blond giggler.

A squeal of joy, followed by a scattering of applause, and the booming voice of Andy in the Afternoon announcing the victory to his listeners.

Finally, Belle stood across the table from Matt.

She looked very serious. And very beautiful.

"I'd like a piece of cheese pizza, please," she said stiffly. She watched while he put it in a triangular cardboard box. When he passed it over, she took it in both hands, as if afraid she might drop it.

"Thank you," she said. "And…Matt…"

He smiled, the exact same smile he'd given the three people in front of her. In his big, booming radio voice, Andy had begun to describe the little blond cutie who had just stepped up for her chance at the diamond ring.

"Yes?"

She took a deep breath. "I'd like to talk to you. I know you don't want to, but…I won't need long. Just a few minutes. When you're finished here, of course."

"Of course," he said politely. He reached down, grabbed a box of Cinnamon Diamonds that had been sitting at his feet, and handed it to her.

"That would be fine. We're done here at six."

BELLE FOUND A BENCH just down the beach from the action, near a broken finger of rocks that jutted out into the Pacific. She took her pizza, and her little box of Cinnamon Diamonds, and set them beside her. She was far too edgy to eat, but maybe she could feed the seagulls.

Oh, no, no. Customer Rejects Diamante Offering…Feeds It to the Birds? What terrible PR that would be!

In spite of her nerves, she had to smile. Maybe she was destined to stay in public relations, after all. She had already begun to think that way.

If she hadn't already ruined her chances. She wondered what Matt had told people about her departure. If he put the word out that she was poison, she wouldn't be able to get a PR job anywhere in California.

The breeze kicked up. At only the end of July, San Francisco had already lost that summer feeling. She put on her sweater and folded her hands in her lap. She ran through her speech once again, trying to find a way to make it better.

But it was what it was. She could only hope that the truth had some little ping that sounded different, like the ring of a fork against true lead crystal. Otherwise, she was sunk. She had only her word for any of it.

If someone had brought her a self-serving story like this, back when she was a reporter, she would never have believed it. Not coming from such a biased source. Not without corroboration. Not without proof.

He didn't come at six. She tried not to worry. She could see them, down the beach, still handing out pizzas to people who had decided to take some home for dinner.

That was desirable, in PR terms. She knew by now that a successful event never ended on time. So she waited, watching the angles of the sunlight grow more extreme. The blue of the water deepened, and patches of green and black formed out where it got deep.

At six-twenty, she saw him walking toward her. Nervous, squirming things came alive in her belly, and she squeezed her muscles tightly, trying to force them into submission.

He'd put on a Windbreaker, and its collar was turned up against his neck. His hair feathered against the fabric, and she clenched her hands, remembering the way the thick, silky strands had felt between her fingers.

She tried not to think what would happen if he didn't believe her. If she had to leave today and never see him, never touch him again.

She knew the odds were against her. But it didn't matter whether he forgave her or not. She'd come because, like her father, she had a secret left to tell.

She had come to tell Matt she loved him.

What happened after that was up to him.

"Hi," he said when he drew near enough to be heard over the wind.

"Hi." She stood awkwardly. "Thanks for coming. I thought…I thought we should talk."

"Yes," he said calmly. He glanced down at the unopened boxes. "You didn't eat your Diamonds."

"No," she said. "I—" She swallowed. "I was too nervous to eat. I have so much to say, and I'm not sure I can explain it in a way you can understand."

He put a foot up on the bench and leaned one elbow on his knee. The wind was behind him, blowing his shining, dark hair over his forehead. "Try me."

"All right." She sat down again. She picked up the box of Cinnamon Diamonds and set it in her lap, just to give her fingers something to fidget with.

"I recognized you the minute I saw you," she said. "I mean, I knew you were…the man I'd met at the Halloween party. But you didn't seem to recognize me, and I hoped that meant you'd never find out."

"Why didn't you just tell me?"

"I don't know," she said honestly. "Sometimes I thought about coming clean, but I felt like such a fool. I'd looked so different that night, and you'd been drinking a lot. I guess I was afraid you might be disappointed. Or disgusted. I was only nineteen, but I was clearly ready to get into bed with the first handsome stranger I met."

"Not the first," he said, and she saw a glint of something in his eyes. "I remember your mentioning a couple of other guys who'd been making passes that night. Put you in a rather foul humor, if I remember correctly."

"Yes, that's true. As I recall, it was a fairly impressive collection of pickup lines."

He smiled. "Well, it was a fairly impressive costume."

"That's the problem. It was a lot more impressive than the real Belle Carson."

He tilted his head. "Depends on what you're measuring, I'd think."

She felt some of the wriggling anxiety subside. That was a very nice thing to say. Perhaps he wasn't as upset as he had been that night. Of course, he was a good-natured person and that outburst had been an aberration. And he probably didn't, in the end, care enough to go around nursing a grudge.

"Anyhow, I wasn't offended by your falling asleep that night. The idea that I'd taken the job for some kind of revenge…it's just impossible. Back then, I was disappointed, of course. But I was also a little relieved. I sort of sensed I was in over my head."

She bit her lower lip. "It was only later that I understood how much I'd lost. It was only later that I realized…"

He shifted his elbow on his knee. "Realized what?"

"That I'd fallen in love with you." She looked at him, refusing to flinch. "I know it sounds insane. And maybe it wasn't really love. But it was…it was something that haunted me from that moment on. It was something I could never feel for any other man."

A couple walked by, and Matt turned his head to the side, to see whether it was someone they knew. His profile was silhouetted against the blue-gold of the early evening sky, and she drank it in, memorizing it. In case she never saw it again.

When they were alone once more, he turned back. "Is that all?"

"No. I want to tell you about the job. I didn't accept it with any hidden motives, Matt. I was mourning the loss of my newspaper dream, I won't deny that. I needed a job, and I wasn't happy to settle for what I thought was second best. But I hadn't been at Diamante a week before I saw…that I could learn to love it."

The setting sun had begun to finger-paint the sky behind him, and it was now so brilliant that Matt's features were hardly visible. He had said very little. She wished she could see his face better, so that she could judge whether there was any point in going on.

Was he just being polite, letting her have closure? Or was he completely coldhearted, allowing her to hang herself with all these unsubstantiated, flimsy protestations of innocence?

Did he even entertain the possibility that she was telling the truth?

And now she'd reached the hardest part. The part where, in order to tell the truth, she had to admit how foolish and selfish, and downright unethical, she'd been.

She took a deep breath of salty air.

"But the part about Todd Kirkland. You were right about that. When David brought me the information and asked me to look into it, I was tempted. I could see how it might be a coup, a chance to impress someone in the newspaper business. I told him I'd poke around. And I did, for one afternoon. And then…"

Matt waited.

"And then I just couldn't do it anymore. I don't want

to be part of covering anything up, and if he was guilty, I'm glad he's gone. But I didn't want to be the one to bring him down. I didn't want to betray your trust."

Matt wasn't looking at her anymore. He plucked at the soft fabric of his jeans, moving it up to be more comfortable.

"It was all true," he said. "Todd had a lot of personal problems. He lost his only child years ago, and it nearly destroyed him. He pulled himself together, but I guess his wife just never could bounce back. He started buying things, trying to bring her out of her depression. Things he couldn't afford. When he got in over his head, he took money from the fund. He'd turn down employee requests for money, but in the books he'd list the request as granted. It wasn't very sophisticated, and it was full of holes. He was bound to get caught, but he was desperate."

"I'm sorry," she said. And she was. A year ago, she might have been more cynical. She'd seen it a dozen times in her journalism career. When a politician got caught taking kickbacks or bribes or slipping his hand into the public kitty, he always had a sob story to tell.

But maybe learning about her grandfather's terrible mistakes had taught Belle something. It had taught her that you could be a decent person and still get tangled up in very bad things.

"We're trying to make it right with every employee he turned down unfairly."

"Yes, I know. David told me. That's generous of you."

"No, it isn't. It's too little too late."

For the first time, she heard how exhausted he was. And she realized that their little interlude was hardly the biggest problem on his plate. Todd Kirkland's betrayal would have been a crisis anytime. Right in the middle of the expansion, it was brutal.

"I should have been more aggressive about checking into the rumors," Matt said, looking off into the distance with tired eyes. "For some of these employees, the crisis we could have helped avert has already done its damage."

She was silent, sure that he wouldn't want empty words of reassurance. She could imagine how guilty he must feel. If she knew one thing about the Malone family, it was that they loved their business and valued its employees.

Suddenly he looked back at her. "Who is David?"

"He's a lawyer—"

"I know what he does for a living. I mean, what is he to you?"

"He was my boyfriend for two years." She fiddled with the Cinnamon Diamonds box. "A few months before I came to work for Diamante, he gave me an ultimatum. Marry him or let him go. I let him go. It was one of the hardest things I've ever done."

"Why? Do you love him?"

"No. But he loves me. Or he did. And I hated to hurt him."

"I see."

She waited another minute, but it was fairly clear he didn't intend to ask her any questions, or share his reaction to her explanation. It was time to put the last card on the table and then go home.

"You see…the other night, when we made love…that was when I gave you my body." She shivered in the rapidly chilling air. Telling the truth was so much harder than playing it safe. "But I gave you my heart eight years ago, and you've had it ever since. I know you didn't ask for it, and you probably don't even want it. Still, the truth is…I love you, Matt. I have for a very long time. And I wanted you to know."

With trembling fingers, she picked up the pizza and the pastries, and smoothed her skirt. She tried to make herself stand.

The seagulls cried around them, probably smelling the uneaten food. The waves broke against the rocks.

She looked at him, willing him to say something before she left. Anything.

To her surprise, he smiled. "You still haven't eaten your Cinnamon Diamonds."

She shook her head, not sure why he cared. Was he just trying to postpone the moment when he had to break her heart?

"No," she said politely. "I'll…I'll save them for later."

"I think you should eat them now."

She felt stupid, her brain heavy with sorrow. Why was he pushing this silly issue? She couldn't imagine eating anything right now.

He took the box out of her hands and opened it. The scent of cinnamon mingled with the sea salt in the air.

"This order was made especially for you, Belle. If you hadn't come here today, I would have delivered it to your apartment tonight."

She glanced into the box, which held the standard Cinnamon Diamond, a small ribbon of sweetness spiraling into a sugary rosette. Beautiful, but meaningless.

It would not even begin to feed the hunger that had hollowed her out since the night he'd left her.

"Belle," he said quietly. "Look inside."

Numbly she picked the pastry up. Unwound it slowly.

Even if it did hold one of the silver plastic rings, why would that matter? The rings had been her idea, and she knew better than anyone how cheap they were, and how plentiful.

And then she saw it.

Not a ring at all.

An earring.

Gaudy, heavy, encrusted with crystal and rhinestone.

Her ear tingled suddenly with the tactile memory of that Halloween night. The way it dragged on her lobe. The way it dangled cold against her neck.

The way it had warmed when he kissed her, pressing it into the pulse at the side of her throat.

She recognized it without a sliver of a doubt. She'd looked at that same filigreed sparkle, encased behind glass above her dresser, for eight years now.

But hers was still at home, buried in shame beneath her thermal leggings and other seldom-needed skiwear. There was no way he could have…

Finally, the truth dawned.

This wasn't hers. This was the match. The other half. The half that had slipped from her ear. The half that she believed had been swallowed up by the crowded hotel ballroom, or the black acres of parking lot, never to be seen again.

"You kept it all these years." She raised her eyes to his. "Why?"

"Because it was all I had left of you."

Her heart began to beat high in her throat. She held the earring tightly in her hand, not caring that the frosting was melting between her fingers, like sugary tears.

"It was all I had," he went on. "And somewhere in the fog of my dumb male brain, I knew you were the best thing that had ever happened to me."

Even the seagulls seemed to have paused overhead, holding their breath.

He hadn't forgotten that night, either. He had known, as she did, that it was something very special.

"And now?" She almost whispered the words. "Do you still feel that way now?"

"More than ever," he said, his voice deep and strangely husky.

She shook her head. "But how—"

"I tried to find you, but no one knew who you were. So, for the past eight years, I've been in love with an idea. A ghost lover. The one that got away."

When he said that, her own palms tingled. She knew so well what he meant. The dream of love lost. The fading echo of the sweetest laughter, always just around the next corner.

"Now I'm in love with the real woman." He reached out and touched her cheek with the back of his hand. "I'm in love with the laughter and the tears. The stubborn pride, the refusal to be cowed. The creativity, the complexity, the charm."

His gaze fell to her lips. "The passion."

"But—" Her mouth tingled as if he'd touched it. "After what you believe I did—"

"You didn't do anything. The things I said to you that night were unforgivable. I wasn't thinking clearly. When we made love, it was so…"

He shook his head. "I've never felt like that. I felt too vulnerable. I had lost control for the first time in my life."

Though the breeze still blew against her face, she felt her cheeks heating, as she remembered the abandon of that moment. He'd seemed so masterful, and then, when it all exploded, she'd been too lost in her own tumbling surrender to realize that he, too, was falling through space, and helpless.

"When I saw the earring, I couldn't quite make sense of it. I thought my memory must be playing tricks on me. I still don't understand how I could have been so stupid. For weeks now, I've been sensing that you had something in common with…with her. But I never made the connection. Until I saw the earring. It hit me then, an avalanche of emotions I was still too drained to process."

It took her breath away, realizing what a fragile thread led a person along the winding path to his destiny.

They might never have made it into the bedroom that night.

And, if she'd realized he still had the match to her earring, she would never have had the nerve to let him enter her apartment at all. Because she didn't know, she'd felt safe. No man, after all these years, would recognize the exact shape and size of a piece of worthless costume jewelry.

And so she'd opened her door, and her heart…and somehow made it possible for this incredible happy ending to find her.

"And then I heard another man at your door, talking about your investigation of Diamante. I...it went through me like a knife. It didn't make any logical sense, but in that moment I believed you had made a fool of me, and then betrayed me."

"Oh, Matt," she breathed. "How could I have—"

He took her face between his hands. "As I said, it was unforgivable. I didn't mean it. Maybe I was subconsciously looking for a way out of a relationship that was too intense to feel safe. But through it all, I loved you. If it's true that you love me...if you can find it in your heart to forgive the unforgivable..."

"I love you," she said. "And I think I could forgive you anything. But this isn't your sin. If I hadn't kept so many secrets..."

He dropped the box, with its loose spirals of forgotten pastry, letting it tumble sideways onto the bench. Then he took her by the shoulders and slowly pulled her in.

With a low murmur, he wrapped his arms around her, tightly, shutting out the evening chill.

"Have all the secrets you want," he said, his lips warm against her ear. "It will be my pleasure to try to coax them out of you."

It was only then, when she heard the playful sensuality in his voice, that she allowed herself to believe it. She laughed softly, and the misery she'd felt since the night he left shook loose and blew away on the darkening breeze.

She felt light enough to float away, too, so she clung to him, anchoring herself in the moment.

She leaned her head against his shoulder, relief and bliss coursing through her. He smelled like cinnamon and sunscreen. He felt like desire and laughter, like hope and home.

She made a small sound, her heart so full she couldn't seem to hold it all in.

He loosened his grip. "Too tight?"

She shook her head. Unable to give the feelings words, she just moved closer. He made her complete. He made her strong.

He made her unafraid to be herself.

"Never," she said. "If it's your arms around me, there's no such thing as too tight."

"Excellent. Because I have a feeling I'm going to keep you pretty close from now on."

"Oh, really?" She smiled, her cheek shifting against his shirt. "To make sure I don't go investigating things on the sly?"

"No." He kissed the top of her head, and heat speared through her. She wondered whose house was closer, his or hers....

"To make sure I don't dress up in sexy costumes and go trolling for strange men in hotel ballrooms?"

"You'd darn well better not," he said with playful heat.

"Well, let's see, then. Perhaps to make sure I don't disappear again, on the stroke of midnight?"

"You may think that's funny," he said. "But I've lost you twice now, Belle. It was...I can't ever go through that again."

"You won't have to."

"Damn right I won't. You see, I know a simple trick. Every night when the clock strikes twelve, I'll make sure I've got you in my arms."

He tightened the hand he had wrapped around her waist. "Like this."

With his other hand, he opened her fist, which she'd closed protectively around the earring. He lifted one frosted finger, put it to his mouth and sucked softly.

"I understand it works best," he explained helpfully, "if we're both completely naked." He thought for a second. "Well. I guess you could wear the earrings."

She laughed, or tried to. But something was burning, deep inside, and it had stolen all her air.

"Tighter," he said softly. In a single motion, he tilted her hips into him, and licked her finger one more fiery time.

She caught her breath. "Like this?"

"Exactly like that. Every night of our lives. And I promise you, sweetheart. The magic will never end."

* * * * *

Don't miss the next book in this family saga!
Look for LIKE FATHER, LIKE SON
by Karina Bliss in November 2009 from
Harlequin Superromance®.

The helicopter swung abruptly sideways in a dizzying arch, setting Jack McCall's fever-ravaged brain spinning.

His friend's voice sounded tinny, coming through the earphones. "You belong in a hospital," he said. "Not some backwater bed-and-breakfast."

All Jack really knew about the virus raging through his system was that it wasn't contagious, and there was no known treatment for it besides a lot of rest and quiet. "I don't like hospitals," he responded, hoping he sounded like his normal self. "They're full of sick people."

Vince Griffin chuckled but it was a dry sound, rough at the edges. "What's in Stone Creek, Arizona?" he asked. "Besides a whole lot of nothin'?"

Ashley O'Ballivan was in Stone Creek, and she was a whole lot of somethin', but Jack had neither the strength nor the inclination to explain. After the way he'd ducked out six months before, he didn't expect a welcome, knew he didn't deserve one. But Ashley, being Ashley, would take him in whatever her misgivings.

He had to get to Ashley; he'd be all right.

He closed his eyes, letting the fever swallow him.

There was no telling how much time had passed

when he became aware of the chopper blades slowing overhead. Dimly, he saw the private ambulance waiting on the airfield outside of Stone Creek; it seemed that twilight had descended.

Jack sighed with relief. His clothes felt clammy against his flesh. His teeth began to chatter as two figures unloaded a gurney from the back of the ambulance and waited for the blades to stop.

"Great," Vince remarked, unsnapping his seat belt. "Those two look like volunteers, not real EMTs."

The chopper bounced sickeningly on its runners, and Vince, with a shake of his head, pushed open his door and jumped to the ground, head down.

Jack waited, wondering if he'd be able to stand on his own. After fumbling unsuccessfully with the buckle on his seat belt, he decided not.

When it was safe the EMTs approached, following Vince, who opened Jack's door.

His old friend Tanner Quinn stepped around Vince, his grin not quite reaching his eyes.

"You look like hell warmed over," he told Jack cheerfully.

"Since when are you an EMT?" Jack retorted.

Tanner reached in, wedged a shoulder under Jack's right arm and hauled him out of the chopper. His knees immediately buckled, and Vince stepped up, supporting him on the other side.

"In a place like Stone Creek," Tanner replied, "everybody helps out."

They reached the wheeled gurney, and Jack found himself on his back.

Tanner and the second man strapped him down, a process that brought back a few bad memories.

"Is there even a hospital in this place?" Vince asked irritably from somewhere in the night.

"There's a pretty good clinic over in Indian Rock," Tanner answered easily, "and it isn't far to Flagstaff." He paused to help his buddy hoist Jack and the gurney into the back of the ambulance. "You're in good hands, Jack. My wife is the best veterinarian in the state."

Jack laughed raggedly at that.

Vince muttered a curse.

Tanner climbed into the back beside him, perched on some kind of fold-down seat. The other man shut the doors.

"You in any pain?" Tanner said as his partner climbed into the driver's seat and started the engine.

"No." Jack looked up at his oldest and closest friend and wished he'd listened to Vince. Ever since he'd come down with the virus—a week after snatching a five-year-old girl back from her non-custodial parent, a small-time Colombian drug dealer—he hadn't been able to think about anyone or anything but Ashley. When he *could* think, anyway.

Now, in one of the first clearheaded moments he'd experienced since checking himself out of Bethesda the day before, he realized he might be making a major mistake. Not by facing Ashley—he owed her that much and a lot more. No, he could be putting her in danger, putting Tanner and his daughter and his pregnant wife in danger, too.

"I shouldn't have come here," he said, keeping his voice low.

Tanner shook his head, his jaw clamped down hard as though he was irritated by Jack's statement.

"This is where you belong," Tanner insisted. "If you'd had sense enough to know that six months ago, old buddy, when you bailed on Ashley without so much as a fare-thee-well, you wouldn't be in this mess."

Ashley. The name had run through his mind a million times in those six months, but hearing somebody say it out loud was like having a fist close around his insides and squeeze hard.

Jack couldn't speak.

Tanner didn't press for further conversation.

The ambulance bumped over country roads, finally hitting smooth blacktop.

"Here we are," Tanner said. "Ashley's place."

* * * * *

Will Jack be able to patch things up with Ashley,
or will his past put the woman he loves
in harm's way?
Find out in
AT HOME IN STONE CREEK
by Linda Lael Miller
Available November 2009 from
Silhouette Special Edition®

This November,
Silhouette Special Edition®
brings you

NEW YORK TIMES
BESTSELLING AUTHOR

LINDA LAEL
MILLER

At Home in
Stone Creek

Available in November
wherever books are sold.

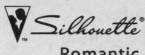

Silhouette®

Romantic
SUSPENSE

*Sparked by Danger,
Fueled by Passion.*

*Blackout
At Christmas*

Beth Cornelison,
Sharron McClellan,
Jennifer Morey

What happens when a major blackout shuts
down the entire Western seaboard on Christmas
Eve? Follow stories of danger, intrigue and
romance as three women learn to trust their
instincts to survive and open their hearts to the
love that unexpectedly comes their way.

*Available November
wherever books are sold.*

Visit Silhouette Books at www.eHarlequin.com

SRS27653

This November,
queen of the rugged rancher

PATRICIA THAYER

teams up with

DONNA ALWARD

*to bring you an extra-special treat
this holiday season—*

*two romantic stories
in one book!*

Join sisters Amelia and Kelley for Christmas at
Rocking H Ranch where these feisty cowgirls swap
presents for proposals, mistletoe for marriage and
experience the unbeatable rush of falling in love!

Available in November wherever books are sold.

www.eHarlequin.com

HR17619

REQUEST YOUR FREE BOOKS!

2 FREE NOVELS PLUS 2 FREE GIFTS!

HARLEQUIN®

Super Romance®

Exciting, emotional, unexpected!

YES! Please send me 2 FREE Harlequin® Superromance® novels and my 2 FREE gifts (gifts are worth about $10). After receiving them, if I don't wish to receive any more books, I can return the shipping statement marked "cancel." If I don't cancel, I will receive 6 brand-new novels every month and be billed just $4.69 per book in the U.S. or $5.24 per book in Canada. That's a savings of close to 15% off the cover price! It's quite a bargain! Shipping and handling is just 50¢ per book*. I understand that accepting the 2 free books and gifts places me under no obligation to buy anything. I can always return a shipment and cancel at any time. Even if I never buy another book from Harlequin, the two free books and gifts are mine to keep forever.

135 HDN EYLG 336 HDN EYLS

Name _____ (PLEASE PRINT) _____

Address _____ Apt. # _____

City _____ State/Prov. _____ Zip/Postal Code _____

Signature (if under 18, a parent or guardian must sign)

Mail to the **Harlequin Reader Service:**
IN U.S.A.: P.O. Box 1867, Buffalo, NY 14240-1867
IN CANADA: P.O. Box 609, Fort Erie, Ontario L2A 5X3

Not valid to current subscribers of Harlequin Superromance books.

Are you a current subscriber of Harlequin Superromance books and want to receive the larger-print edition?
Call 1-800-873-8635 today!

* Terms and prices subject to change without notice. Prices do not include applicable taxes. Sales tax applicable in N.Y. Canadian residents will be charged applicable provincial taxes and GST. Offer not valid in Quebec. This offer is limited to one order per household. All orders subject to approval. Credit or debit balances in a customer's account(s) may be offset by any other outstanding balance owed by or to the customer. Please allow 4 to 6 weeks for delivery. Offer available while quantities last.

Your Privacy: Harlequin is committed to protecting your privacy. Our Privacy Policy is available online at www.eHarlequin.com or upon request from the Reader Service. From time to time we make our lists of customers available to reputable third parties who may have a product or service of interest to you. If you would prefer we not share your name and address, please check here. ☐

HSR09R

Silhouette Desire

**FROM *NEW YORK TIMES*
BESTSELLING AUTHOR**

DIANA
PALMER

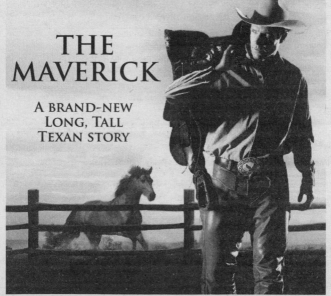

THE
MAVERICK

**A BRAND-NEW
LONG, TALL
TEXAN STORY**

x

Visit Silhouette Books at www.eHarlequin.com

x

SD76982

HARLEQUIN® Super Romance®

COMING NEXT MONTH

Available November 10, 2009

#1596 LIKE FATHER, LIKE SON • Karina Bliss
The Diamond Legacy
What's worse? Discovering his heritage is a lie or following in his grandfather's footsteps? All Joe Fraser *does* know is that Philippa Browne is pregnant and he's got to do right by her. Too bad she has her own ideas about motherhood…and marriage

#1597 HER SECRET RIVAL • Abby Gaines
Those Merritt Girls
Taking over her father's law firm isn't just the professional opportunity of a lifetime—it's a chance for Megan Merritt to finally get close to him. Winning a lucrative divorce case is her way to prove she's the one for the job. Except the opposing lawyer in the divorce is Travis Jamieson, who is also after her dad's job!

#1598 A CONFLICT OF INTEREST • Anna Adams
Welcome to Honesty
Jake Sloane knows right from wrong—as a judge, it's his responsibility. Until he meets Maria Keaton, he's never blurred that line. Now his attraction to her is tearing him between what his head knows he should do and what his heart wants.

#1599 HOME FOR THE HOLIDAYS • Sarah Mayberry
Single Father
Raising his kids on his own is a huge learning curve for Joe Lawson. So does he really have time to fall for the unconventional woman next door, Hannah Napier? Time or not that's what's happening….

#1600 A MAN WORTH LOVING • Kimberly Van Meter
Home in Emmett's Mill
Aubrey Rose can't stand Sammy Halvorsen when they first meet. She agrees to be a nanny to his infant son only because she's a sucker for babies. As she gets to know Sammy, however, she starts to fall for him. But how to make him realize he's a man worth loving?

#1601 UNEXPECTED GIFTS • Holly Jacobs
9 Months Later
Elinore Cartright has her hands full overseeing the teen parenting program, especially when she discovers *she's* unexpectedly expecting. Not how she envisioned her forties, but life's unpredictable. So is her friend Zac Keller, who suddenly wants to date her *and* be a daddy, too!

HSRCNMBPA1009